THE COCKTAIL OF LOVE

THE COCKTAIL OF LOVE

DHRUV MALOO

Srishti
PUBLISHERS & DISTRIBUTORS

Srishti Publishers & Distributors
A unit of AJR Publishing LLP
212A, Peacock Lane
Shahpur Jat, New Delhi – 110 049
editorial@srishtipublishers.com

First published by
Srishti Publishers & Distributors in 2021

10 9 8 7 6 5 4

Printed and bound in India

For the Almighty,
My family,
My late sister Meenal.

Acknowledgement

A writer never embarks on the journey of becoming an author alone. A lot of helping hands and support systems are with the writer on this journey. For my journey, I would like to thank everyone who has been so supportive.

My parents Arvind Maloo, Rashmi Maloo, and my brother Devesh Maloo for supporting my dream all through the years with patience, and always motivating me, no matter what.

Mr Sunil Mantri and Mr Surjit Verma for their undeterred faith in me, along with their continuous efforts and guidance, without which this book would still just be a file on my laptop.

Ms Sunita Sharma for always encouraging me with my writing endeavours in my school days.

Ms Tulsi Negi for lending immense support in the initial days of this book.

Rashi Shrivastava for being an initial critic and playing a pivotal role in improving the flow of the story.

Bharat Khurana for always being there to help, in anything that I asked for.

Gauri Gupta and Tasneem Amiruddin for coming up with such an impressive cover.

Himansh Chawla for the author photograph.

The brilliant team at Srishti Publishers for giving life to the story and turning it into a book. Especially, Arup Bose, for showing utmost faith in my story and making me comfortable at every step of the publishing process. Stuti, for always being there to address all my doubts, queries and providing solutions to everything. Vini Bhati, for impeccably editing the manuscript and making it more captivating and worth reading. I can't imagine this book coming to life without Srishti.

The wonderful group of friends and people around me who have always inspired me.

Prologue

Samar

It had been more than five minutes of stirring my cup of espresso. The whirls that had formed in the cup had fanned my curiosity.

How familiar they seemed to the current state of my mind as I struggled with a storm created by my own thoughts and circumstances. Maira, unaware of the misery that she had inflicted upon me, reclined comfortably in a chair across the table, slurping a fresh pineapple juice and eating a delectable bruschetta.

'Samar, I guess now we are friends, right?' she asked me, after we had spent almost an hour discussing Mumbai. Our interaction mostly revolved around its attributes – people, food, places to visit and an apparent cultural diversification it exhibited, in comparison to Delhi.

'Of course, we are friends,' I said with an honest grin and she understood.

We talked some more and since we were friends now, I even tried to dig into her bruschetta playfully. However, she retracted it in time, projecting a wicked yet friendly smirk on her face.

I felt grateful to her for asking me out for this meeting. I pretended to have succumbed to her persuasion, but I had longed for this change. Her jovial and amiable persona had helped me come out of the cocoon that I had lately constructed around myself. We were able to establish a rapport as soon as we had met.

My reluctance to meet her since she was a friend of *hers* had now faded entirely. It was just our second meeting, yet we seemed to share a lot in common. It could have continued that way, had she not intervened to ask.

'So, now that we are friends, you won't mind anything I ask you, right?'

'Umm, okay,' I shrugged, wearing a smile, totally unaware of the situation I was about to face.

'Okay, so tell me about the two of you. I know that you might think that she has already told me everything about you people, but she hasn't. I want to hear your side of the story,' she spoke, leaving me stunned.

I already knew that Maira was her friend. In fact, now when I was out of *her* life, Maira was perhaps the closest to her. But, Maira wasn't my friend until a few minutes ago. I agreed to us being friends because she caught me in the moment, and perhaps out of etiquette.

I answered in the affirmative nonetheless. I didn't foresee that she would expect me to share my life story with her in the second meeting itself.

Moreover, I had come to Mumbai to take a break. A break from Maira's 'friend'! However, now that she had mentioned her, my break was over.

'Umm,' I couldn't think of a reply and sought refuge in stirring my coffee.

'Samar, you just said we are friends. And, I don't think it's good to hide things from your friends,' she said, gently placing her hand on mine.

Her touch was very comforting. Still, I couldn't utter a word. I chose not to. Although my wounds were in the process of healing, revealing anything to Maira could render them open. I wasn't ready for that.

'It's okay. I know it must be hard for you to trust me. I think it was wrong on my part. I shouldn't have asked you this in the first place. I am sorry,' she said sweetly.

As I heard her words, I felt miserable. She had tried to lend me a shoulder, but I shut her down. Her words made me feel very guilty. I knew for a fact that I needed to vent out my feelings. I wondered if confiding in Maira could help me do it. She seemed to be the right person at the moment.

'No, I trust you. That's why I think I should tell you everything,' I said.

'Really?' she turned towards me, pleased with my answer. 'You can always count on me, Samar,' she said, tightening her grip on my hand to give me assurance.

'What do you want to know?' I replied, giving in to her.

'Everything!' she said, with a strong emphasis.

I thought for a few seconds, wondering where to start. Which incident was the most significant?

After struggling with a few thoughts, I finalized the most important event.

'It was our graduation dinner,' I began.

❖

Ashna

On the thirteenth day after the accident, I woke up with the stench of turmeric milk filling up my nose.

I found my mother sitting beside my bed, holding a glass of yellow milk, perhaps her way of ensuring that I heal soon. I cringed, but she made me drink it anyway. While I was at it, I figured out that I didn't want to spend another day in confusion. This thought continued till I gulped down the entire milk.

Thereafter, though unintentionally, I started playing with the ring on my finger. The same ring that someone had recently given me.

The sudden realization that understanding profound sentiments like love and friendship isn't a cakewalk was quite overwhelming. Some people take years to finally realize what they want in life.

I didn't want to be one of them. I had to make a very critical decision, which is why I decided to adopt a meticulous approach. I wanted to carefully consider the pros and cons of every possibility.

Of course, my diary could help me figure out what I wanted!

I thought about it a little more and immediately asked my mother to bring it from my cupboard. As soon as she brought it, I opened it and flipped through the pages, nostalgia running through my head.

Finally, my eyes stopped on a page that had recorded in words the event that changed the course of my life. If I were to make an informed decision, I had to revisit the most defining episode of my life.

The Graduation Dinner!

1

Taking the Leap

Samar

I checked myself for the umpteenth time in the side view mirror of a car parked outside the college party hall. My black tux looked immaculate and my hair was neatly styled, which radiated a very formal vibe. I was confident that I looked perfect for the occasion.

However, I was still nervous because I knew that merely looking good would not suffice for what I had planned. After much consideration, I had decided to do something that I had never done before. I had to ensure that everything went well.

After giving myself a small pep talk, I climbed the stairs to the entrance of the party hall.

GRADUATION 2014

The banner greeted me at the entrance of the hall, which was filled with smartly-dressed people. Men looked dapper in their formal suits and women looked equally ravishing in their gorgeous sarees.

The hall was lit up with multicoloured lights flickering at regular intervals, creating a discotheque ambience. People were either grooving to the latest dance numbers or relishing the exquisite delicacies from the college canteen's kitchen, which was a rare sight in regular days.

The entire affair was arranged by our college to celebrate our graduation. That night was officially the last time we had come to college as students. Thereafter, we would be the alumni. Thus, everyone wanted to live in the moment, as they were soaking in the pleasures of their carefree days. For me, that night was way more significant than just food or dancing. I was ready to take the leap.

Remember what Bollywood has always taught us? A guy and a girl can never be *just friends*.

Well! Ashna and I had been friends from the first week of our college. At first, we were just two classmates who didn't even talk to each other because I had been too shy to talk to the pretty girl who was sitting next to me.

But she had managed to break the ice between us. During one of the lectures, she casually passed me a book, sneaking in a note which said, 'Hey!'

If you are given a choice between a pretty girl and a bespectacled middle-aged, partially bald man who is continuously asking you to focus on the board, whom would you listen to?

You guessed it right! I chose to talk to her.

That one conversation became the starting point of a strong and fulfilling friendship, and eventually, we became best friends. Not just regular best friends but inseparable buddies like Jai and Aditi in the movie *Jaane Tu... Ya Jaane Na*. It was tough for me to spend even a single day without her. The most beautiful part of our friendship was our unequivocal commitment towards each other. We knew that we were there to hold each other's hands during desperate circumstances.

However, when my mind and heart messed up with each other, my life took a filmi turn. I don't know when or how, but I fell head-over-heels in love with her.

In spite of being aware of my situation, I could never bring myself to confess my feelings. The fear of losing her prevented me from confessing my love to her.

But tonight, I had decided to surpass all my apprehensions and insecurities. After all, it was my last chance! I decided that no matter what, I would propose to her.

I began searching for her in the party hall, around the dance area and the buffet. She was nowhere to be seen. I almost thought that she wasn't there when I felt somebody's hand on my shoulder from behind.

'Samar?'

It was a familiar voice. I turned around, delighted to see my friend Kartik.

'Thank god, you found me, bro!' I said with a sigh of relief and hugged him.

'Dude, you are killing it today. Your hairstyle looks terrific. What have you styled it with? Wax?' Kartik said as he shook my hand.

We believed that we were past the age of fist bumps, so we made handshakes our thing.

'Thanks bro! But, which year is this, 2002? Who uses wax now? I got them set,' I replied as I ruffled my hair straight above my forehead.

'By the way, you look gorgeous as well.' I grinned.

'Gorgeous? Really? Is that a compliment you want to give me?' he asked with a disgusted face and playfully punched me in my gut. I smirked at him.

'By the way Samar, how did that thing go? According to plan?'

I realised what he was referring to. 'I haven't found her yet. Have you, by any chance, seen her in the party tonight?'

'When are you planning to tell her then?' he asked, clearly annoyed.

Kartik was one of my closest friends. He was more like Dr Watson to my Sherlock or Ron to my Harry.

Apart from being a dedicated friend, he was also a relationship counsellor to me. I shared everything with him. It was his approval that had given me the strength to proceed with the proposal.

'I am still not sure,' I said, with a little hesitation. Even though I really wanted to, I was sceptical about this.

'Please tell me you are joking. We've spent almost two-and-a-half hours discussing *the plan,* and now you are saying that you still have doubts? What is this fear that holds you back every time you decide to confess your feelings?'

'It's the fear of losing her,' I replied softly.

'I understand Samar, but it is irrational. Why do you always assume that you will lose her? She is your best friend. It's all about the chemistry that you people share,' he replied in a low voice.

'What if this chemistry doesn't exist in real? What if it is just my assumption?' I asked thoughtfully.

'Mr Socrates! From where do you bring up these lines? See, this is not the first time I am telling you this. But certainly, this is the last time you can tell her about your feelings. From tomorrow onwards, our lives will change. All you have is tonight. Just go and get her!' Kartik exhorted.

That restored faith in me. That's why I was relieved to see him, because I knew he would clear all my doubts.

I took a sigh that the Spartans must have taken before going to the battle.

'Okay! I will do it,' I said confidently.

Kartik gave me a pat on my back and I proceeded to accomplish my goal. I looked almost everywhere inside the party hall, and even in the parking space outside. I even waited for her for almost ten minutes outside the girl's washroom, tolerating all the weird looks I received, but she didn't turn up.

When you plan for something so diligently in life, even a small hindrance can cause an overbearing sense of despair and hopelessness.

I too had started to feel despondent. I became restless and my mind started to ponder all pessimistic scenarios.

Why wasn't she around?

What if she has already left?

What if she got to know about my feelings and decided to maintain distance from me?

What if someone else already asked her out and she accepted it?

My irrational thoughts terrorized me. The jovial environment of the party started to suffocate me.

2

The Magic of Destiny

Samar

From the time my mind and heart accepted the existence of romance, I believed that someday, my destiny will enable me to cross paths with my soul mate.

My philosophy materialized when I met Ashna – my best friend. I was sure she was my soul mate.

When I didn't find her in the party hall on the night of the farewell, I decided to leave. But whenever I tried to leave, small events unfolded, which compelled me to stay. This was destiny playing its cards. I was about to leave when a spotlight fell on the other entrance of the hall. Soon enough, I realized that the spotlight marked the beginning of a fashion show.

All the participants looked gorgeous, but the showstopper was someone in a black saree. As she walked into the hall, all eyes were glued to her. She had long, flowing hair and her skin was radiant. The elegance with which she carried that black saree made her look like a stylish diva.

When I turned to see her, my dismal mood was revived in an instant. There she was – my hope, my aspiration, my life and most importantly, my best friend.

Oh! Not that diva in the black saree, but the girl behind her.

She stood elegantly draped in a crimson red saree with a golden border. She had a simple yet the prettiest face that projected innocence and purity. Her hair was blowing in the air, away from her face, while the curly ends rested casually on her shoulders. Her smile was the solution to my problems. She was Ashna.

While all others were busy noticing the show stopper, for me, every other participant ceased to exist, the very moment Ashna entered the realm. As soon as the show got over, I walked over to her.

'Samar!' she exclaimed as she saw me approaching.

I could clearly see a gush of excitement surfacing on her face. That's how she always was, bubbly and chirpy. She would always get thrilled when I was around her. She ruffled my hair playfully and I liked it.

'Where were you?' she asked, feigning an angry expression. And then, she stooped in towards me for a hug. I turned slightly towards the right and gave her a side hug. Even though we had shared almost everything with each other, our hugs were jinxed. I could never embrace her properly in a hug, no matter how badly I wanted to.

'I'll tell you everything. But first, you have to come with me,' I said and clutched her hand softly.

She followed me. 'Okay, but where?' she asked me, clearly puzzled at my behaviour.

'Just come with me,' I said and didn't leave her hand till we left the party hall. We started walking on the pathway beside the college ground.

'Ahem ahem,' she cleared her throat to tease me. 'Samar, what is your intention?' she gave me a crooked smile and a naughty wink.

'Any guesses?'

'Please! Tell me where we are going? You know I don't like it when you hide things from me,' she said in a childlike tone.

'Just wait for a few minutes Ashna,' I said as I pinched her plump cheeks lovingly.

My heart pounded faster than usual in trepidation as we neared the designated spot. It was next to the basketball court, across the college ground. I was experiencing a mix of exhilaration and nervousness. With each step, my tension rose.

Be positive! My mind instructed.

'Ashna, before we reach that place, there is something that I want to give you,' I spoke as I put my hand into the inner pocket of my coat to fetch the first surprise gift of that evening. I gave a pocket-sized notebook to her. It was a flipbook, one that created the visual of a moving picture when its pages were flipped in rapid motion.

I had designed it a few months ago and wanted to give it as a birthday present to Ashna. But, it was too hard for me to wait for that long. So I had decided to give it to her that night, as a part of the plan.

'What is this?' she asked curiously, her face brightening up on seeing it.

'Just flip the pages and you will figure out what it is,' I replied.

'Wow! This is so sweet of you,' she said blissfully as she read the title "The Sunshine" and the phrase "Starring Samar and Ashna" below it.

She couldn't wait any longer and hurriedly flipped the pages of that pocket book, just as I had directed. A small picture came to life. The visual time was just three seconds and I had tried to project 'our' story in that limited time.

Seems impossible, right? Well, I had somehow pulled it off.

As she flipped the pages, the first image that came across was that of two illustrated characters - Samar and Ashna.

The cartoon story began with the two of them standing at a distance. The gap between them receded as the pages were flipped. The two characters came closer to each other, eventually holding each other's hand. This illustrated how at first, we were strangers who became friends and gradually grew emotionally attached to each other.

Going further, the figure of Samar embraced the figure of Ashna and finally, she rested her head on his shoulder. This portrayed what the future looked like for us. She turned over to the last page and read the message which I had written to give the pocket book a proper ending:

To the friend I love the most.

'Did you like it?' I asked Ashna as she closed the book and clutched it close to her heart.

She looked intently at me. Without saying anything, she came closer to me. She rested her head against my shoulder, closing her eyes; just as I had depicted in that flipbook.

'Samar, you are the best thing that has ever happened to me,' she said after a few seconds.

'Please promise me that you will always remain my best friend,' she spoke slowly, in a heavy voice.

'Ashna,' I said. She turned to look at me. I cupped her face in my hands and said, 'Of course, I will always be there for you. Forever.'

She smiled and wiped off a tiny drop of tear from the corner of her eye.

'If you have become so emotional just by looking at this small surprise, then I don't know how you'll feel when I show you the rest.'

'Wow! There's more? Samar! Are you part-time Santa?' she exclaimed.

'Yeah! Just for you. Now, stop asking me questions and follow me,' I replied with a pleasant smile on my face.

'Why are we heading towards the basketball court? Don't tell me you want to play basketball now. Seriously, I won't be able to play in a saree,' Ashna said, as she raised her eyebrows in amusement.

'Yes, I want to play the last game of our college life,' I replied to her naivety in a sarcastic manner.

'What? Are you ma… '

'Shh!' I interrupted her by placing my finger on her lips. We reached the intended spot.

Let's roll! I mentally boosted myself. 'We are not going to the basketball court. So relax and just close your eyes,' I said.

'For what?' she asked, clearly puzzled by what lay ahead.

'Do you really have to ask all these questions? Why can't you just do what I say?' I asked her, feigning disappointment on my face.

'All right, I am closing my eyes. Don't get angry at me,' she said, making a puppy face and closing her eyes right away.

'When I tell you to, only then can you open your eyes,' I said, looking at her face while I performed the final touches of my grand show.

'Open your eyes now,' I said, after everything was ready to be executed.

As soon as she opened her eyes, her glance rested on me. I gestured her to look upwards. She was clearly captivated by the spectacle that I had orchestrated and her jaw dropped in amazement. Both of us stood under a peepal tree which was illuminated with the light of various lanterns that hung on different branches. The warm light from the lanterns had engulfed the surrounding darkness. The tree looked surreal. Everything seemed unblemished, like a well-crafted scene.

I kept looking at Ashna as she seemed to be absorbing the beauty of that moment. I was elated to see the joy that

Ashna's face radiated, looking at the lanterns. Even though she didn't say anything, she just looked at me with gleaming eyes and a captivating smile.

I always knew that she wanted a fairy-tale proposal. Since she seemed to like it, I decided to move ahead for one last thing. Without any delay, I got down on one knee.

'Ashna!' I called her name.

She turned her face towards me, baffled. Before she could say anything, I carefully took out a dried peepal leaf from my coat's outer pocket and handed it over to her.

She observed the leaf carefully and read the message which I had engraved on it. It said,

You are most precious to me and I want to keep you forever. I have always loved you and I always will.

She was stunned and kept looking at it for a while. She didn't say anything, not even a single word. Her eyes were stuck on the leaf. Her silence was unnerving, but I chose to keep my calm.

'I have just asked you out, Ashna' I said, slowly rising up and taking hold of the situation.

'Samar!' she finally uttered something, looking down at her feet. 'I need some time to think about it.'

What? Think? About what? We have been together for the past four years. And now she needs time to think about it. Oh god! My mind was brimming with these thoughts but I chose to keep quiet.

Time was slipping out of hand and I had no idea what to do.

I almost died of a panic attack in my head. My surprise proposal had backfired.

'Okay, take your time. I am always here for you, Ashna.'

I replied as I let go of her hand. She walked away slowly, avoiding any eye contact with me.

I remained transfixed under the peepal tree, but somehow the glow from the lanterns didn't seem warm anymore.

3

The Decision

Ashna

I lay on my bed, twisting and turning for almost two hours. I couldn't sleep a wink. The only reason why sleep eluded me was Samar. I wanted to believe that whatever happened that night was just a figment of my imagination.

Getting a proposal from your best friend was a very baffling situation. Before giving him an answer, I wanted to understand my feelings better. The trajectory of my relationship with Samar depended entirely on my decision.

'Damn!' I exclaimed and stood up from the bed, exasperated. Had it been about someone else, I would have turned to Samar and he would have sailed me smoothly through it. However, since I could not do that, I called up my second-best friend, Sakshi.

Before Samar had become a part of my life, Sakshi was the one with whom I used to share everything. But gradually, I became closer to Samar and started finding solace in his company. However, Sakshi and I were still pretty close and spoke regularly. As I was experiencing a very puzzling dilemma, I knew Sakshi would be able to give me some insights and perspective.

With the same thought in mind, I decided to talk to her, not realizing it was 3 a.m.

'Hello, Sakshi?' I asked.

'Obviously, who else would pick up my phone at this hour?' she replied in an irritated and sleepy voice.

'Of course! So what were you doing?' I asked.

'Are you kidding me! Did you wake me up at 3 a.m. to have random chit chat? This better be important Ashna!' she spoke, clearly irritated at my behaviour.

'Samar proposed to me,' I blurted out spontaneously.

Although I had thought of revealing this news after a random conversation, I couldn't hide it any longer.

'What?' she shouted in amazement.

'Yes, can you imagine that? Samar has proposed to *me*? Unbelievable, right?' I said shockingly.

'Unbelievable?' she asked and giggled. 'You know what's unbelievable? After all these years, he has finally gathered the courage to tell you that he likes you,' she said, leaving me utterly confused.

She knew about this? If she did, then how come I never saw it?

My mind raised a number of questions.

'You knew about his feelings? Did he tell you?' I finally managed to ask her.

'Yeah obviously, I knew about it. In fact, everybody did. It was so easy to tell,' she spoke in a matter-of-fact manner.

'If it was so easy to tell, then how come I didn't notice it?' I spoke, slowly coming to terms with the truth.

'Because you were always ignorant about it. His feelings towards you were always crystal clear. The way he cared for you, the way he fulfilled your wishes and most importantly, how he considered you to be the most important person of his life. Isn't it obvious?' she said.

Sakshi's words made a lot of sense. Perhaps I had been ignorant about Samar's feelings towards me.

'Okay, just tell me what is your answer? Are you going to—' She was halfway when I interrupted her.

'I don't know, Sakshi!'

'What do you mean *you don't know*? It's either a yes or a no,' she emphasised.

'Sakshi, it's not that simple for me. You already know how important he is to me, *as a friend*. My decision, either way, will change the course of our relationship. I am not sure what I want,' I said, sounding perplexed.

'So, is that why you have called me up in the middle of the night? Because you want to be sure about your own feelings and you need me to help you with that?' she said.

'Yeah and I also want you to tell me what to do,' I said, voicing my helplessness quite clearly.

'You and Samar have always been too involved with each other. It seems as if you both already are in a relationship. Then, what's the problem?' she asked, in an exasperated tone.

'I know we have been involved with each other, but it's only because he is my best friend. I haven't imagined him to be more than that. It's not as if I am romantically inclined towards him. In fact, if he wouldn't have proposed, I could have never imagined what was on his mind!' I said, trying my best to explain my conflict to Sakshi.

'See Ashna, you are the one who's always saying that Samar is the best. Then, what is the problem in dating a guy who's so good?'

'Yes, he is indeed the best. But I have never thought of dating him! How can I make up my mind all of a sudden?' I said. My head started to feel heavy due to this complex conundrum.

'Do you think you will ever be able to get a guy who will understand you better than him? He knows everything about you. In fact, I think you should give this relationship a try!' she said.

'Sakshi, I do love him, but just as a friend. And, what if I never fall in love with him? Won't it destroy our friendship forever?' I wanted her to understand why I feared blurring these lines between friendship and love. I wasn't sure whether I would ever understand that distinction.

'Stop speculating so much Ashna. All you need to do is to focus on the fact that you are happiest around him. I think you should consider this and give him a chance. I am sure you will definitely fall in love with him someday!' she spoke with a sense of conviction.

'But—' I was about to say something when she intervened.

'Sshh! Just do as I say because you know that I can't be wrong about you. Now, please stop bothering me and let me sleep.'

'Okay, I guess you are right. I won't be able to know if I don't even give it a try. I know I can count on your advice. Thanks a lot. I hope you face some kind of crisis soon so that I too can help you out of it,' I said and giggled, trying to lighten my mood.

After I hung up, I tried to sleep. I thought about whatever Sakshi had said. Everything seemed logical. But I still had doubts.

However, as morning approached, all my doubts had withered away and I reached a conclusion.

How was I supposed to tell Samar? I didn't want any confrontation with him.

4

The Unexpected News

Samar

Samar,

I thought about last night, and I must confess to you that I could have never imagined that you could be so romantic. Surely, it was something beyond imagination. A perfect and fairy tale proposal! Something I have only dreamt about till now. I am sure that any other girl would have given up everything to get into my shoes, because it was the best a girl could have.

I was in the middle of a letter that Ashna had given to Divish, my younger brother, when she had suddenly dropped by my house, early in the morning. I should have known that Ashna would prefer writing a letter instead of telling me directly. Whenever she had something important to say, she preferred to say it in writing, rather than confronting that person directly.

I possessed a stack of letters written by Ashna on various occasions, throughout our college life. Whether it was the 'I-was-not-wrong-you-were' letter, or the 'I-am-really-sorry' letter, or the 'I-have-a-big-secret-to-tell-you' letter, I had a type of every letter that one person could possibly write to another.

However, the letter that I had received that morning was different. That letter may have contained my happiness, something which I had longed for almost four years.

As far as I had read the letter, it was apparent that Ashna was in awe of my proposal. She had absolutely loved it. So, without even reading it further, I knew that her answer was 'yes'.

I wanted to read those exact words that comprised her feelings for me. Hence, I read further.

Nobody could have done it except you. But, I am really sorry Samar. I can't feel for you the way you feel for me, maybe because you are my best friend. I know that you love me and you have been by my side through every phase of life, supporting me whenever I felt alone. I really appreciate that, but I can't love you more than a friend. You will always remain my most favourite person. I love you as a friend, but I cannot complicate things between us. I always want my best friend with me, so I will always need you by my side. I can't afford to lose you because you are a part of me. If I lose you, I lose everything.

Please try to understand.
Ashna

Upon finishing the letter, my mind experienced a sense of shock. The ecstasy that I had felt a few moments ago vanished all of a sudden. I read the letter again, and then two times more, but the words didn't change. It was hard to digest the fact that I was rejected by my best friend.

'She didn't love me! Then, what was all that between us all these years? What about all the moments we shared? What about everything I did for her? Why did she always tell me that I was the most important person for her, if this wasn't love? If my best friend, who had shared every bit of her life with me, did not love me, then who would? Was I such a jerk?'

These thoughts created a storm in my head. I felt inferior. Perhaps, I had expected too much, and now when she had rejected me, I felt as though there was some problem with me. I felt as if I was not good enough for her. Not good enough for anybody, for that matter.

I walked over to the balcony just to stand there and gaze at the sky. I had many questions for Ashna, but nothing was the same as before.

I rested my elbows on the railing and looked up at the tranquil sky which was in stark contrast to my chaotic heart.

I tried to think deeply, putting myself in Ashna's shoes but it was impossible for me to look at her as just my best friend. My mind kept wandering to the beautiful moments that I had spent with her, which intensified the frustration of being rejected.

I needed an emotional support so I decided to call Kartik. Only a good friend could lend me moral support at a time like that.

'Hello,' I said in a grave voice as soon as Kartik answered the call.

'Hello? Samar? Why do you sound as if your ass has taken a real beating from somebody?' he asked, unaware of the tormenting situation I had just faced.

I sighed. 'Samar, what's the matter?' he asked, this time with more sincerity.

I heaved another sigh and continued in the same grave tone, 'Ashna, she rejected me.'

'Why? Did she give you a reason?' he questioned, exasperation dripping from his tone.

I narrated the ordeal that I had gone through. By the end of it, Kartik could feel my pain.

'Are you still going to talk to her? Even after all this?' he asked curiously.

'Yes! Why shouldn't I? She is still my best friend,' I replied confidently.

'Are you out of your mind? Do you want to remain friend-zoned forever? You know what, I think you are too attached to the I-love-Ashna-fuck-my-career philosophy,' Kartik said enraged.

I had never seen him so angry before. Somewhere in my mind, I knew that he was right. I had wasted a lot of time trying to make Ashna fall in love with me. But, this had to stop now.

'She is one of the most important persons in my life. I can't walk out on her just like that. I don't want to,' I spoke sincerely, sounding like some die-hard rom-com hero. 'Wait!

I have another strategy. This will definitely work,' I said and smirked happily.

'Another strategy? Are you totally nuts? I hope you realize that you are an adult. It's important for you to focus on your career instead of making strategies to woo a girl. Grow up, man!' Kartik said.

'I want her by my side. If not as a girlfriend then, as a friend,' I completed my statement with a sense of satisfaction.

We were about to carry our conversation further when suddenly, I heard dad calling out my name. He was coming into my room. I disconnected the call and hastily hid the phone underneath my bed sheet, standing next to my study table.

I could sense that something important was coming my way as both mom and dad paraded in together.

'What are you doing?' Dad asked, scanning my room critically to check that their six-pointer son wasn't wasting his time.

'Nothing much, I was just reading some books,' I replied, grabbing any book from the study table and waving it in the air just to make him see it.

I neither had a rich, orthodox and disciplinarian father who would impose his opinions on me; nor a social butterfly mother who didn't give me enough attention. My parents were not like these movie prototypes.

We were a simple middle-class family. My father owned a decent business and my mother was a homemaker. They had always cared for me and supported me through thick and thin. They expected a stable career from me, just like any other middle-class parents do. And in spite of everything they had done, their son couldn't clear even a single job interview in the campus placement of his college.

'Not yet? Then, what are your plans for the future? You didn't get placed due to low grades, so please tell us what you are going to do with your life?' my mom asked me angrily.

'Mom, I didn't get placed because I didn't want that job,' I said with confidence. 'I have planned something big for myself. I have decided to continue with my passion for drawing cartoons and take it up as a career,' I said, looking at them for their responses.

'Cartooning?' Dad responded with a gasp as if he had caught me drinking from his bottle of scotch.

'Yes, what's the problem?' I asked, enlarging my eyes. 'You already know how passionate I am for cartooning, and now, I really want to pursue it professionally.'

'How can you be so unreasonable? Did you study architecture to be a cartoonist? Why did you spend my money on this architecture course?' Dad said, bombarding me with an array of questions.

I didn't have any answers. Sensing my apprehensions, he calmed down.

'Okay,' Dad began, 'since you have taken this insane decision to be a cartoonist, then become one. We have never forced our choices on you and we won't in future too.'

I was shocked that I didn't get slapped for my absurd request.

'But,' he said and I turned back towards him, looking confused. 'We are giving you three months. In these three months, you either find a permanent job as a cartoonist or at least get your cartoons published in magazines or newspapers as a freelancer. And if you fail to do so, then without any questions and excuses, you will have to join my business,' Dad said and left the room.

All this while, I had been hoping for some help from my mother since she had been very supportive. When she followed Dad out of the room, reality became clearer to me.

I understood that their decision was final as they had run out of patience. Left alone in my room, I found myself engaging with a series of thoughts. First, my best friend had rejected me. Second, I had no stable job. And finally, I had an ultimatum from my parents.

Where is my life going?

I thought and stupidly looked up for an answer, but god didn't have any customer care service.

5

The New Beginning

Ashna

Tick tock. Tick tock.

I could hear the ticking of the wall clock; reminding me that time did not stop.

I knew that Samar had received my letter, as Divish told me. Samar hadn't talked to me for the entire day, but it felt like eternity. He hadn't answered any of my ten calls and eighty-six WhatsApp messages.

Even though Sakshi had almost convinced me to accept Samar's proposal, I couldn't follow her advice. I couldn't force my heart to feel anything for him and I didn't want to pretend.

Deep down, I knew that Samar deserved someone better. Someone who could understand his feelings, and value how caring, kind, loving, truthful and passionate he was. Unlike me, who claimed to be his best friend, but didn't have the slightest idea of what he harboured in his heart all along.

I checked my phone after every few minutes to see whether he was online on WhatsApp or not. I was so desperate to talk to him that every time I heard any notification, I rushed and looked at my phone, hoping that finally he might have messaged.

But, he didn't.

When my phone buzzed an hour or so later, I didn't pay much heed to it. However, soon, a sense of hope urged me to check my phone, thinking that it could be a message from Samar.

To my utter misfortune, there was no message from him. Instead, it was an e-mail.

'BIZTECH,' I read the first word excitedly. I quickly opened the mail and read it further.

Dear Ms Ashna,

In reference to the job offer email dated 15 January 2014, confirming your selection for the position of Junior Architect with Biztech, we would like to welcome you to the Biztech team.

We are excited to have you and looking forward to working with you beginning from 1 July 2014.

I hopped with joy, like a bunny pacing up and down my house. Biztech was one of the leading architectural companies in Delhi. I had cracked all the interviews during the campus recruitment. But even after four months, I had not received any confirmation on the joining date. Finally, after an endless wait, Biztech had shared my joining date in an official mail.

My family was thrilled when they heard the good news. They were proud of my accomplishment and made it a point to celebrate it with my most favourite dish, *Ras malai.*

Everyone got the news of my achievement, except Samar. I wanted to share my happiness with him. However, he wasn't answering my calls. He had helped me prepare for the interview. In fact, when I had been busy with a cousin's wedding, Samar had prepared my resume. When I had cracked the interview, he had been as delighted as my parents were. Naturally, I wanted to celebrate this moment with him, but he was busy being egoistic.

Was all that really a big deal for him? Did his feelings become more important to him than us?

Since he was not picking up my calls. I decided to call on his mother's number.

'Hello,' I said nervously. I could feel my heartbeat racing against my chest and my ears went numb.

'Who's that?' she replied, her voice crisp.

'Na... Namaste aunty, I am Ashna,' I introduced myself.

'Namaste beta! How are you?' she asked politely.

'I'm fine aunty, what about you?' I continued, hoping that the conversation would continue smoothly.

'I am good,' she replied curtly.

'Is Samar around, aunty?' I said, coming to the point directly by avoiding any kind of small talk.

'Samar? Yeah, just a moment,' she said, after taking a pause for a few seconds. 'No beta, Samar is not around.

I think he has gone out. Why don't you try to call on his number?' she continued.

I figured out that Samar was around, but he had instructed his mother to tell me that he wasn't at home.

'Oh, I tried, but he did not attend his calls. That's why I called on your number,' I replied hesitantly.

'Okay beta, was there something important that you wanted to talk to him about? You can tell me if you want to. I will let him know when he comes back,' she said, sounding a little curious and interrogative.

'No, no, nothing special aunty,' I said and giggled awkwardly. 'I just wanted to tell him that I received a confirmation from Biztech. I have to join office from July,' I said, sounding chirpy.

'Oh, wow! That's great news beta. Congratulations!' she said. I didn't understand why she emphasized on the word 'congratulations' more. Maybe she wanted Samar to hear or maybe I was over-thinking. 'I will definitely tell Samar about this when he comes back,' she said.

We ended the call after some formal salutations. I felt relieved. I wasn't surprised to see Samar's WhatsApp just some minutes after I hung up. I felt happy.

Samar
Congrats.
Ashna
Hmm thanks.
Samar
Hmm? What happened?

Ashna

Wow! As if you don't know.

Samar

Ok, I know, but leave that for now. You must be excited? Finally, your dream will get fulfilled.

Ashna

Yeah.

Samar

What yeah?

Ashna

Yeah, it's good, but why do you care?

Samar

Why are you talking like this?

Ashna

Because you are being formal.

Samar

I am not.

Ashna

Yes, you are.

Samar

This is how I talk to friends.

Ashna

Sure, as if I don't know how you talk to friends. See Samar, I am sorry. I really am, but please try to understand.

Samar

It's okay. Please don't explain anything.

Ashna

No, I want to. You know that you are a great guy Samar and you will definitely find someone better. In fact, you 'deserve' someone better. I am not right for you.

Samar

Let's not talk about this. And, I don't want someone better. I just want what I want.

Ashna

So, are you going to keep talking to me like this?

Samar

No, I am sorry Ashna.

Ashna

Please Samar, I am sorry for being a pathetic person. How could I not feel the way you feel for me? You are the best person I've known, and you are my best friend. I've always hurt you. I don't deserve a friend like you. I know you hate me now. But please forgive me! ☹

Samar

Shut up Ashna. Don't say sorry. It was not your fault. You never said that you felt more than a friend for me. It was my fault. I tried to force my feelings on you and that was wrong. Then I overreacted and behaved like a total jerk and stopped talking to you.

Ashna

Are you mad? You know that it's my fault. Being your best friend I should have known about this a long time ago or I should have felt the way you feel for me, but I can't Samar. I have failed you, and you won't stop being nice to me. Why are you so nice?

Samar

I am not as nice as you think I am. It's just that our friendship is important to me, more than anything else.

Ashna

Samar, why can't I be nice like you? Why can't I reciprocate your feelings? Why can't I give you the happiness you deserve?

Samar

Some feelings can't be forced Ashna. You can't make yourself fall in love with me, even if you try. So it's not your fault. Just chill!

Ashna

I can't, till you get normal. I don't want to lose you. Even though I know I won't, still the mere thought of it gives me shivers down my spine.

Samar

Ashna, we are good now. Don't worry, you won't lose me. I won't let you go.

Ashna

No, not like this. You have to promise me that whatever happens in the future, you will never stop talking to me.

Samar

You know that you don't need to take this promise from me. We will always remain the same.

Ashna

Promise me Samar.

Samar

Oho, okay, I promise you.

I knew that his feelings wouldn't wither away in a day, but eventually they would.

I was on the top of the world. My best friend was back with me. I had my dream job, and my parents were proud and happy.

What else could I have asked for! Everything was just perfect. But, little had I known that this wasn't going to last for too long.

Samar

It's high time, Samar. When will you learn, if not now?? When will you start thinking about yourself? When will you become responsible and mature? Next year, you will be 25, but look at you! You haven't even figured out what you want from life. Stop! Buck up and do something!

These series of questions were not launched at me either by my extremely concerned parents or my comforting friend Kartik.

It was me, confronting the handsome guy in the mirror.

When you are twenty-four, unemployed and you have no clue about your life, anxiety gets the better of you. That was exactly what was happening with me.

As I was engaging with my troubled mind in a very dramatic style, Divish overheard me. Curiosity took the better of him and he banged the door to see if everything was fine. I instantly unbolted the door as I didn't want him or anyone to know my plight. Obviously, they weren't going to believe that I was merely gazing at the mirror and boosting my morale.

I silently moved away and settled onto my bed, plugging in the earphones. Trying to seek some distraction, I decided to watch an English sit-com which happened to be about an architect who was fired from a big project. What was he supposed to do now? Interestingly, his crises mirrored my life struggle.

As Divish saw me, deeply immersed in my phone, he said something gesturing towards me.

'What? Did you say something?' I asked removing one of my buds.

'I just want to know whether you are over Ashna or do you still have hopes that she might reciprocate your love someday?' he said and looked at me with his eyebrows raised.

'How do you know that she has rejected me?' I enquired. I had no clue how Divish knew about my proposal and also her answer.

'I overheard it when you were talking, sorry, whining about it with Kartik,' he replied in a matter of fact manner. 'I know she is your best friend and you love her very much, but who cries like that?'

'I wasn't crying.' I snickered, trying to maintain my poker face.

'Bhai, tell me something! Why is it so important for you to get her approval? Is there a guarantee that she will stay in your life forever? You people have just started your careers. Who knows where your life will take you? Do you really think you need a serious relationship with her at the moment?' he asked, looking at me intently.

I was pretty impressed by his wisdom.

'I understand what you are trying to say. I will think about it,' I said, trying to avert his philosophical advice.

'Good! By the way, I have good news for you. In fact, a job offer,' he continued.

'What kind of a job?' I asked, plugging back one of the buds into my ear so that it partly conveyed that I wasn't interested in his offer.

'Our company is looking for cartoonists for a new marketing gimmick,' he said, looking at me.

'Your company deals in medicines. How can you people relate cartoons with medicines?' I asked inquisitively.

'We want to market our app digitally on social media platforms like Facebook, Twitter and Instagram. We were thinking of incorporating illustrations into our campaign. I think you can do that easily. This is a great opportunity. I can talk to my HR team if you are willing to take this up,' he spoke sincerely.

I didn't reply for a long time. Maybe I wanted to think it through.

'I think you should take this job,' he continued. 'Otherwise, you won't have anything to excuse yourself from dad's three-month challenge. Whenever you decide, just let me know and I'll arrange an interview for you,' he said as he swiftly gathered his things and left.

Divish's offer was good. The job was related to cartooning and it could easily get me through that three-month challenge. However, it wasn't the perfect option for me. I did not want to settle for anything, especially when I was beginning my career. Most importantly, this job wouldn't match the standard of Ashna's job at Biztech. Hence, I decided to decline the job offer, but I abstained from saying this to Divish right away.

Getting up from my bed, I cleared my study table. I put a pencil box with different shades of pencils, colours, some inspiring comic books and everything else that a cartoonist might need in order to create a masterpiece. I even asked mom to prepare me a cup of coffee.

Creative people always perform these customary rituals before getting started with their work. I thought, pleased at the very sight of the table.

I placed a drawing sheet at the centre of the table and kept my cup of coffee on one end.

'Now what? I have to think of a design!' I mumbled to myself.

I pushed the boundaries of my imagination to come up with a path-breaking idea, literally putting all my body weight on the backrest of the chair, till it tilted a little. My hands were entwined behind my head and I stared at a wall in front of me. I almost feigned myself to be an artist, looking at his muse for inspiration. However, nothing constructive came to my mind.

I took a pencil in my hand and decided to do some random sketching. I was hoping that some noteworthy illustration would organically emerge from those sketches. I drew lines, lips, curves, eyes and everything else that I could think of. They were cartoons, line drawings and still figures, but they were not what I wanted. All of them were bland, as if devoid of a soul.

This was supposed to be an easy task, then why am I not able to make any good cartoons?

Maybe I was over-confident. Then how did I manage to make that flipbook for Ashna?

Did I lose my creative instincts?

6

Office Adventures

Ashna

'Here is your coffee,' said Maira, gently placing a cup on my messy desk as she stood beside my chair, leaning her haunches against my table.

She stared at me, intermittently sipping from her own cup that she held firmly in her hands. Perhaps, I did look like a workaholic zombie!

My fingers typed endlessly and my eyes were strictly glued to the screen of my laptop.

'Get a break, girl,' she said, forcefully shutting down my laptop.

I knew I had no time for breaks as life had turned hectic for me. It had been more than two months since I had joined Biztech, but I was still struggling to get acquainted with work pressure. Researches, reports and presentations occupied my entire day, leaving me immensely exhausted.

Only calls and messages from Samar kept me rejuvenated and made me look forward to life. It felt nice to talk to him.

Maira, my colleague, was more a friend to me than a bossy and demanding senior. She became my confidante, replacing Sakshi, who went to Bengaluru to pursue her MBA. As we got busy with our respective lives, we couldn't talk every day.

Perhaps, such changes are a part of growing up. As we move forward in life, things and people who once mattered a lot become less important.

Maira had become an integral part of my life even before I had realized it. Her friendly and caring nature had played an important part in solidifying our connection. She knew almost everything about me, even about Samar. However, she never shared much about her personal life. All I knew was that she belonged to a financially well off family and had a married elder brother who stayed abroad.

'I am done,' I said, gulping down my coffee.

'I don't have even a minute to spare now. Aman will kill me if I don't give this report to him by the end of the day.'

'Nah, he won't,' she said in a relaxed tone. She moved towards her desk but returned to my desk after a few minutes. I figured out that she had something important to discuss.

I was about to say something when she interrupted, 'Did Samar ever try to propose to you again?' she asked with a curious face, totally out of the blue. 'Or did he mention or try to convey that he loves you, again?'

'Why are you asking this, all of a sudden?' I enquired. The question felt like a breach of my privacy.

'Curiosity,' she said, making an innocent face.

'No, he did not propose to me again. Samar knows that we are best friends and our relationship doesn't need any other definition. Now tell me, why did you ask me this, Maira?

'I was just thinking, what if he is not yet over you? What if he is just pretending so that things between you and him don't get complicated? I mean, one can't really know what's going on in someone's mind,' she spoke thoughtfully.

'I am sure he is over me and has moved on,' I said, feeling confident of my connection with Samar.

'Okay, maybe I was wrong. But what about you? Are you sure that you don't love him now or will fall for him in future?'

'Of course, I am sure. We are just good friends. Who falls in love with their best friend, Maira?' I was exasperated at what Maira was thinking.

'A lot of people actually do,' she remarked, giggling to herself.

'Maybe, but I am definitely not one of those people. By the way, why are you so interested in knowing whether Samar is still into me or not? Do you really wish Samar to not be interested in me?' I asked, narrowing my eyes at her.

'Please Ashna, don't tell me you think I am interested in him! No! Even though he seems to be utterly romantic and cute,' she said bluntly.

'Okay, okay it's your decision. You are letting a gem slip out of your hands. Anyway, if you are done gossiping, may I go back to my work?' I said, clearly annoyed.

'I don't understand how you are always working so much! Why don't you relax sometime?' she continued, clearly not interested in working.

'Wow! Being my senior, you should be far more worried than me about work. You are answerable to Aman if I do not complete my work. But this hardly bothers you. How do you manage to stay so relaxed all the time?' I looked at her enquiringly.

'Simple! I don't take a lot of stress,' she said. 'And, Aman is not as devilish as you think he is. He is a sweet guy,' she continued after a brief pause.

'I didn't mean to say that he is a devil. He helped me a lot during my training period when he was my mentor. But you know, he is extremely professional and hard working. That's why he was able to become the manager at such a young age. I just think that he likes to get his work done on time. That's why other people call him by that name,' I replied, giving her a plausible explanation.

'Don't listen to what others have to say. Tell me, has he ever been mean to you? Has he ever mistreated you?' she started questioning me.

'No,' I replied.

'Hitler!' Rajat interjected our conversation, mouthing as he came out of Aman's cubicle. 'He is calling you again Maira,' he said addressing her.

Maira frowned a little. She didn't like how Aman was referred to as Hitler at office. She would instantly jump to his rescue when others would say mean things about him.

I strongly believed that she had some feelings towards him. And that he was also attracted to her.

From the very beginning, I noticed that Aman would often call Maira into his cubicle, sometimes even unnecessarily. He would often find ways to talk to her in the corridor, cafeteria or wherever he found her. Maira too, would look more happy and energetic around him. Something was brewing up between them.

'Ashna, I wanted to ask you something,' Rajat interjected my thoughts. I nodded, gesturing him to carry on.

'Will you go out for lunch with me?' he asked, with a blush on his face.

Did he just ask me out on a date? Was Samar right about Rajat? I thought, my hyperactive mind processing things at an inimitable speed.

'What?' I uttered, stunned at the offer.

'Lunch,' he said, looking confused. 'Will you go out with me?'

'How can you just ask me out for lunch like that?' I retorted, amazed at his audacity.

'Why? Is there anything wrong in having lunch with me?' he jerked back, clearly confused at my reaction.

'There is nothing wrong, but why would you ask me to have lunch with you?

'Because… I didn't bring my tiffin box today,' he replied vaguely, looking at me with a strange expression.

'I thought it would be okay for us to go to the canteen for lunch. If Maira would have been around, I would have invited her as well,' he said smiling at me. It was clear that he understood my reaction.

I looked at him baffled and embarrassed to my core.

Stupid! I thought to myself, biting my lip as I thought of a quick recovery from that awkward situation.

'No, no it's fine. I didn't realize what I was saying, never mind,' I trailed off. 'Let's go!' I said, giving my best smile and inwardly hating myself for being so judgmental.

He reciprocated with a smile and we got up to move to the cafeteria. Just then, we found Aman and Maira approaching us.

'Headed for lunch?' Aman asked, sounding casual.

'Yes sir, please join us,' I said promptly.

'No, you people carry on. I just wanted to talk about an upcoming project. I have briefed Maira about it and wanted to discuss with you two, but you can come to my cubicle after having lunch,' said Aman.

'Sir, we can have our lunch later. Let's talk about the project first,' Rajat said and looked at me for approval.

'Yes sir, let's talk about the project first,' I said and nodded at all of them.

'Great! I am happy to see your enthusiasm which is exactly what we need here at Biztech,' he said and started walking ahead, the three of us in tow.

❖

Aman's cubicle was impeccable. Though it was small, it had everything to inspire me to achieve great heights. The triangular name plate which had his senior position designation written on it spoke volumes about of his hard work and dedication.

Aman settled in his chair and directed us to make ourselves comfortable. After consulting some files on his desk, he started speaking.

'Our company recently closed a deal with Vericon Builders. They want us to design their new hotel in Kausani. Even though it's a small project, we never say no to anything at Biztech. So, right now, our team has the responsibility to coordinate with their representatives and present our ideas to them. We will have to monitor the work. But before all that, we have a meeting with their project manager on the coming Wednesday. I want all of you to join me for that. I think it will be great for our collective growth.'

We were delighted. It was a great opportunity indeed!

I couldn't wait for the meeting. I had already started imagining myself, standing in a fancy office and talking to the clients. But soon, a ping on my PC broke my reverie.

I looked at the screen. There was an official email from Biztech which said that since I was the newest recruit to the team, I was selected to accompany the manager to Kausani, a week after the meeting. It was a rule that the new employees accompany the manager on new projects so that they can have better exposure of client interactions.

My excitement was substituted by nervousness. Even though I was looking forward to the opportunity, I had no rapport with Aman.

How will I ever get through this?

7

The Impromptu Kasauni Plan

Samar

Café Cheeros in Hudson Lane was our regular hangout joint. Even though Hudson Lane had an array of pocket-friendly cafes, Café Cheeros was our favourite. It had embraced every mood of our college years. We had celebrated birthdays, studied for exams and had endlessly gossiped while relishing the famous Mac and Cheese. It was more like The Central Perk to us F.R.I.E.N.D.S!

I stood at the entrance, next to the stairs that led to the first floor. Ashna had asked me to meet her there. She wanted to discuss something about her office and she needed my opinion on that. Lately, she had been very busy with work, which is why we couldn't meet very often. I was so thrilled to meet her that I reached early. To know how much more time she would take, I called her.

'Where are you Ashna?'

'On my way. Will reach in five.'

I didn't mind waiting a little longer for her. I could wait for her for as long as she wanted. Generally, during our meetings, I was the one who always made her wait which annoyed her, but I loved the 'Samar-I-am-fed-up-of-you' expression on her face. I knew that she was someone who didn't wait for anybody else.

Since she was running late and I had some free time, I decided to sit inside the cafe. Almost all the tables were occupied except the one besides their waffle baking counter.

Wow! Today is definitely a lucky day. What a treat to meet Ashna with the aroma of freshly-baked waffles! I contemplated, basking in the aroma already.

I settled myself and ordered their signature Tiramisu shake. I decided to spend time by doodling randomly on a coloured notepad that was placed at the table for customer feedback.

After a while, I ended up drawing an illustration, somehow exactly as I had envisioned it. The sketch had a door at the centre and two people, a woman and a man, sitting equidistantly at each end. Both of them were thinking with their eyes glued to the door, waiting for each other.

Sometimes we shut our doors to the people we love for trivial reasons. We are so consumed by our ego that we end up waiting for them to open the door and make things right. What if the person at the other end is also waiting for the same thing? What if the door never opens?

I was extremely pleased with myself for the marvel that I had created. It was a marvel for me, in spite of technical flaws. The jinx was broken. I had regained my creative instinct.

'What are you doing?' A pleasant voice broke my introspection. I looked up to find Ashna standing there with a smile on her face.

'Hey!' I stood up and gave her the ritualistic side hug. 'Finally you are here,' I said, with a gleaming face.

While she was settling down, I quickly tried to shove the sketch in my pocket. I didn't want Ashna to see it yet.

'Show me what you have made,' she said, grabbing that paper from my hand before I could keep it in my pocket.

'Ashna! No, give it back to me,' I said, but by that time, she had already taken it.

Before she could see it closely, someone called out to her from the entrance. We turned in unison, to see a lean guy standing at the door. Ashna smiled back and gestured him to come over.

'Samar-Rajat,' Ashna introduced us, quite formally.

I knew who Rajat was. He was the office guy who supposedly liked Ashna. I felt a sudden surge of anger inside me. I felt like punching him for no reason. These thoughts were not in my control. Had we been in a relationship, I would not have felt insecure at all. But we weren't, so I always feared that someday, someone would steal her from me. That's why I freaked out on seeing Rajat.

He was far better looking than me. He wasn't muscular, but his broad shoulders and six feet height overshadowed the five-feet-eight-inched me.

What is he doing here, and who invited him? I thought, before forwarding my hand to him for a handshake. However,

I didn't let anything show on my face. I cordially shook his hand and asked him to sit down.

'Samar, you know what, we got late because of this guy,' Ashna began to speak, all cheered up, perhaps on seeing Rajat.

'First, he was willing to accompany us, and then he kept us waiting for almost forty-five minutes,' she said, deliberately emphasising on forty-five minutes. She looked at him angrily for a second, and then grinned.

I didn't find it funny. I was fuming inside and her grin had aggravated it.

Why has she invited him? This was supposed to be our personal meeting. This is our place. How can she invite a third person? And she didn't just invite him; she kept me waiting because he was running late. These weird thoughts made me want to punch him in the face, even though I knew that if we were to be in a combat, he could knock me out.

In my anger, I retracted the sketch from Ashna's side of the table, crumbled it in my fist, and put it back on the table subtly. Somebody had stolen its thunder.

'Sorry, I didn't want you people to wait, but Aman gave me some extra work which needed to be completed today itself,' he said. 'I'm sorry Samar had to wait because of me,' he said, making an apologetic face.

'It is fine, and please don't say sorry,' I said, trying to compose myself.

'Thanks bro!' said Rajat, bro-zoning me in that instant, like we Delhiites usually do. I acknowledged it with a fake smile.

'Are you into business or a job?' he spoke after an awkward pause, choosing the only topic I wasn't comfortable to talk about.

'I am also an architect, and currently I am looking for a job,' I was about to say this when suddenly his phone buzzed taking away our attention.

'Sorry, I need to take this. Excuse me,' he said, looking at the screen. Within minutes, he zoomed out and we could hear his voice fading out as he descended the stairs.

I hope he doesn't come back, I thought totally unaware of how childish my prayers were.

Ashna moved from the chair on my right to the chair across me.

'Show me that sketch, where is it?' she asked, looking for it on the table.

'I threw it away,' I said, looking away from her. Of course, I hadn't thrown it away. It lay there crumbled, in the shape of a table tennis ball, next to the salt and pepper holder. There was a chance that she might have not noticed it, thinking it to be another used tissue.

'Why did you throw it away? I wanted to see it,' she said in a low voice, clearly disappointed. However, she sensed from my reply that something was wrong, 'Is something wrong, Samar?' she asked, very softly.

'No, what would happen?' I said bluntly, pretending that everything was fine.

'Something has definitely happened. Are you angry because I came late?' she asked, with her eyebrows raised and a worried look on her face.

'No, I told you I am not angry,' I replied flatly.

'Shut up! I can tell it from your face. Just tell me what's wrong?' she asked, looking directly at me.

I didn't respond. Instead, I took out my phone to check it randomly. She snatched my phone and said, 'Answer my question! We're meeting after so many days and yet, you are looking so annoyed,' she shouted, almost throwing a tantrum.

'You know that Rajat likes you and still you brought him along here at Cheeros, our special place. Also, we are meeting after almost one week. What do you expect from me? Should I be happy about this?' I blurted out all at once.

She was taken aback. 'So, you are angry because I came with Rajat?' she spurted in an acerbic tone.

I didn't say anything. I just looked away.

'What is wrong with you? You never behaved this way before,' she said.

I realized that there was a sudden change in her voice. I looked at her and noticed that she was overwhelmed.

'You know that I love... I mean, like you,' I said hesitatingly. This uneasiness often engulfed my words whenever I wanted to confess my feelings.

'That's why I feel possessive and insecure about you,' I said softly.

'Samar, why don't you understand that Rajat is just a friend? And, it's not that I was left with a choice because when he got to know that Maira and I were coming here, he requested on tagging along. Obviously, I couldn't say no to him as Maira was also coming. When we reached here, Maira saw some handbags down at the market, so she stayed there to purchase them while I came upstairs with Rajat. Maira should be here any minute,' she said, looking at me with moist eyes.

I felt terrible when I realized how I had accused her. 'Sorry, I know I shouldn't have—' I was about to clarify when a female voice interrupted us.

'Hey!' that girl addressed Ashna. I looked up to see who it was. She had a very beautiful face and a very attractive personality. She had her hair tied in a loose bun, which looked very trendy. Elegantly dressed in her formal attire, she was magnificent. But above else, it was her deep blue-green eyes behind retro cat-eye spectacles that captivated me the most. They were the most beautiful eyes I had ever seen. Had I not been in love with Ashna, I would have definitely tried to hit on her.

'Maira! Didn't you buy anything?' enquired Ashna.

'I bought a turquoise and golden handbag. It's in Rajat's car. I will show you when we head out,' said Maira, sitting down on a chair to my right. Rajat followed in behind her and chose a chair across Maira.

'Hi Samar, I have heard a lot about you,' Maira introduced herself and shook my hand.

Ashna talks about you all the time. I think I may fall in love with her best friend, if she doesn't stop talking about him in the office,' she said, giggling and making me blush. I felt elated hearing that Ashna talked about me with her friends. Maira seemed to be a very warm and confident person. She had a very pleasant aura.

Soon after, we ordered some food after which I excused myself to go to the restroom.The food was already served when I returned to the table. I realized that my sketch was missing from the table. It was gone! Perhaps, the waiter took it away assuming that it was a waste tissue.

After we had finished with our meal, it was time for Rajat and Maira to leave. We said goodbye to them and then silently sat opposite each other. I wanted to talk to Ashna and apologize for what I had said earlier, but I knew her anger hadn't dissipated.

'Till when are you going to feel possessive for me?' she blurted out, addressing me directly. 'Please tell me, so that we can figure out a way to deal with this,' she stated.

'No Ashna, I promise I won't repeat this behaviour. We are best friends and I should not feel possessive for you,' I said, meaning it as a promise, even though I knew that I wouldn't be able to control my feelings for her.

'That's exactly what I am saying,' she said, her voice now mellowed. 'I am not going anywhere. I will always be here, next to you. Best friends stay together, forever,' she said at last.

I believed in whatever she said and felt calm and delighted. 'Even if you want to go away, I won't let you go. I will follow you like that pug in that network commercial,' I said, delving deep into her eyes as my passion overwhelmed my senses.

'Anyway, you had called me here to talk about something?' I asked, checking myself from being carried away by my feelings.

'Oh yes,' she continued, remembering what she had to share. 'Actually, I recently got an opportunity to accompany my manager, Aman for a trip to Kasauni to inspect one hotel site,' she said, sounding excited.

'Great! What's the problem?' I asked her.

'See, as a rule, only new employees get to accompany the manager, which implies that Maira and Rajat won't be joining us. I am still in my learning phase, and I am not experienced enough to use my knowledge at the client site. I am feeling anxious. Plus, what if I make a mistake? I don't even know Aman well enough to ask questions or discuss things with him,' she said, wearing a worried look on her face.

'Ashna you are a confident and hardworking person. You won't make any mistake. Don't miss this opportunity. I'm sure you will end up benefiting a lot from this experience,' I said, trying to cajole her into taking a decision to advance her career.

'I know that. But I am a little sceptical. I feel there is a lot that I have to learn. And then I haven't interacted much with Aman, except for the time I had to assist him. Going to Kausani with him is an altogether different issue.

We got to thinking of a solution. Finally, I came up with a mind-blowing idea.

'Ashna, we can do one thing,' I said, my face lightening up with the idea.

'I can come with you to Kausani. It will be a good outing for us and you'll have moral support, even if things go wrong,' I said, soon realizing that this would be our first outstation trip together.

'Are you kidding? How can you just come? What will you tell your parents?' she asked, bombarding question after question at me. Perhaps, she too was as excited as I was.

'You don't have to worry about it. Just tell me if it's okay for you!' I replied, already planning the trip in my head.

'I love your plan! What can be better than you accompanying me on this trip,' she said, slowly and then brightening up. 'I just love how you always come up with best solutions to all my problems,' she continued, her words proving how happy she was.

First solo trip with Ashna! My heart leapt with joy.

8

The Meeting

Ashna

I was at Hotel Royal Plaza, dressed up in an olive green skater dress paired with my mom's silver vintage earrings. I felt like those high-profile businesswomen who meet at lavish restaurants to discuss important business deals.

We sat in the Lutyens restaurant, and by *we* I mean Aman and I. Rajat and Maira were supposed to accompany us, but didn't show up. Aman told me that Maira had taken a detour to office to pick up some design brochures. Rajat had been stuck in traffic for the past one hour. So they might probably reach in an hour or two. I was a little annoyed at both of them. If I knew about their delays, I would have come late as well. At least that would have saved me from this awkward situation of making small talk with my boss.

Surprisingly, that day Aman was a different person. He greeted me courteously and asked me to join him when we first met in the lobby of that hotel. Not just that, at the table, he even pulled out a chair for me, like a gentleman. He complimented me, saying I looked fabulous. When we were seated at last, he initiated the conversation and assured me that everything would work out just fine. I liked how he made me comfortable.

'I think we both are well prepared for the meeting, so why don't we talk about something else for now?' he spoke in a casual tone. There was an unusual blush on his cheeks.

'There are few points that I need to revise in my presentation,' I said, looking down at my laptop, wondering what else to talk about apart from work.

'Your presentation is absolutely fine, Ashna,' he replied. Before I could say something, he continued, 'You know what, my dad always said that we should not prepare for any exam right before entering the examination hall because then, we forget even what we already know.'

I smiled in response to that cliché knowledge he had just showered upon me. I was about to say something further when he interjected me,

'The boss is always right! No more questions about work,' he continued, laughing heartily.

'Of course sir, but this is my first meeting and I don't want to leave any stone unturned,' I replied in haste. I didn't want him to interrupt me again.

'You have done everything you could possibly do Ashna, trust me,' he said with the pleasant look on his face.

I found everything to be a little out of place.

Maybe he wants to bond with me because I am Maira's friend, and that perhaps, I will tell her nice things about him.

My mind was pondering over all the possibilities. I decided to support the young man in his adventurous quest for Maira.

'If you believe in me, then it must be right,' I said, shutting down my laptop. However, it was hard to find topics to discuss with him.

'Ashna, we never got a chance to know each other,' he said with an endearing expression on his face.

'With all that work pressure in the office, I don't think we will ever get time to bond. So, tell me something about yourself,' he continued.

I had no idea what he wanted to know about me. Also, I didn't know where to begin, so with the confused face, I asked him, 'Like what?'

'Anything like about your family, your friends, your interests, or maybe what food you love. Anything that defines you,' he replied.

I was surprised to see how Aman wanted to know me so well, just to get to Maira. For the next one hour, we discussed various topics. Initially, I was a bit reluctant to open up to him. We talked about politics and movies. However, when I was comfortable, we switched over to some personal topics.

He wanted to know how I was feeling with Biztech and what my expectations from life were. Most of the conversation was about me. It was not because he was reluctant to share, but because he had more questions for me than I had for him.

It was past the time of our meeting with the clients of Vericon Builders. Neither the clients nor Maira and Rajat had showed up.

'Sir, shouldn't everyone have arrived by now?' I asked.

He looked up at me surprised, probably because I had abruptly ended our conversation. Then he looked at his watch and nodded, 'Yes, they should have. Let me just call them and ask,' he said and moved out of the restaurant.

Meanwhile, I decided to text Maira and ask her where she and Rajat were. I saw that she had recently changed her display picture on WhatsApp. Out of curiosity, I zoomed in to have a closer look at it. A little girl in a yellow frock was standing with a lovely smile. She looked adorable. I understood that it was a picture from her childhood. But surprisingly, she had cropped it. Somebody who stood at her side was cut out of the frame. Only the hand of the person was visible.

'Ashna, Vericon has cancelled the meeting for today. We will have to rearrange it a few days later,' he said, looking unperturbed.

'What?' I asked. 'How could they cancel the meeting at the last moment?'

'They had prior commitments,' he replied.

I didn't understand how he seemed so calm. I was miffed. We had worked so hard for the past few days. This was supposed to be my first meeting. I had been so thrilled, but those pricks took away my moment of thunder without any plausible explanation.

Sensing my uneasiness, Aman continued, 'Ashna, the clients are almost like gods to us. We have no other option but to heed to their demands.'

Aman noticed the disappointment on my face and tried to cheer me up by making me excited about future endeavours. He asked to me to inform Rajat and Maira about the meeting, so I did as directed.

I was ready to leave when he said, 'At least we can have lunch before leaving. We have already paid for it.'

I was not in a mood to eat. However, I thought it would be rude to deny his request. After all, he was my boss.

We had lunch together. To cheer me up, Aman shared some of his experiences of meetings where he had been ditched. Aman had a decent sense of humour, something which I wasn't aware of. All this while, I kept thinking how perfect this situation would have been for Maira. Perhaps, this could have become their first date.

After lunch, we moved out of the hotel. Aman offered to drop me to the nearest metro station. In his car, awkwardness emerged between us once again.

Aman broke the ice. 'Tell me something more about you Ashna?'

This question was getting irritating now. I felt as if he was interviewing me all over again so I decided to reply vaguely, 'Haha! I have told you almost everything sir, I don't think anything is left now.'

'I must say that's the minimum that I have heard on this subject,' he said glancing at me with a smile. After a pause he continued, 'Would you mind if I ask you something personal?'

What should I answer to that? Should I say yes or no? You are taking too much time to think, Ashna. Say something. Say anything.

My head processed these thoughts while I thought of a befitting reply.

'Sure,' I replied meekly though my mind had warned me against it.

'Have you ever been in a relationship?' he asked me, clearly very awkwardly.

I should have understood when he said 'personal'. I felt uneasy, so I couldn't answer him right away.

He sensed my discomfort and said, 'You must be thinking why am I asking you this. Actually, I like someone and I don't know how to approach her. So, I thought that I could ask you for help,' he said, smiling nervously.

Maira, of course! I thought. I was thrilled because I wanted him to confess his feelings to Maira. Aman had just given me a chance to be a part of their story.

'Sir, I have never been in a relationship. I don't know whether I will be of much help to you, but I can definitely give you the girl's perspective,' I said very confidently.

'Yes, yes that's what I want,' he said, getting all excited.

'Okay, have you told her yet? I mean, does she know that you like her?' I enquired.

'No, she doesn't, but I plan to tell her soon,' he replied blushing. 'Tell me how should I go about this? I like her very much. What if she freaks out, or is not ready to get into a commitment?' he asked, looking directly into my eyes.

'Sir, you cannot just guess that. At least she needs to know how you feel in order to decide further,' I replied, spilling out my relationship advice like a pro.

'What if she doesn't like me or she likes someone else?' he continued. 'Already no one likes me in the office. I guess I am too bossy,' he replied, perhaps in a sad tone.

'It's not like that, sir. Many people like you. And about that girl, how can you know whether she likes you or not if you don't tell her?' I continued.

'Okay, thank you Ashna,' he said and stopped the car. I realized that we had reached the metro station.

I was about to step out of the car when he said, 'Ashna, I like you,' he said.

I was shocked. 'I am sorry, what?' I cut back at him.

'It's you Ashna. You are that girl I was talking about. The girl I like,' he said as I froze. I couldn't respond.

'I don't know when it happened, but I just started liking you and have been waiting to tell you for a long time. It's just that I got a chance today,' he continued, looking at me directly.

'We don't even know each other properly and this is the first time we have actually spoken to each other,' I said, still unsure of what he had said.

'I totally agree with you, but you're so special. It's hard not to like you. You are so focused and dedicated. Anyone can fall in love with you,' he said.

I couldn't believe that this was actually happening. Have I turned into some kind of a fairy that suddenly every guy wants to be with me?

'Look, I know I am coming a little strong here, but there is no pressure on you,' he said, sensing how quiet I was.

'I don't know what to say,' I said. I was worried about how Maira would feel when I tell her that Aman had asked me out.

'You can take your time Ashna, and believe me, this won't affect our professional relationship at all,' he said and left.

I was in a dilemma. Once again, I had no clue how to proceed.

❖

What are you going to do Ashna? How will you turn down Aman? Wait, saying no to him shouldn't be much of an issue, he seems sensible and hopefully will understand. Let's just assume that he will. But then, how will you explain this situation to Maira?

Seated on a bench at the metro station platform, I tried to think of a solution.

Aman's confession had caught me off guard. Suddenly, everything I had perceived until then, changed drastically. I was sure that Aman and Maira had liked each other and Rajat was the one who probably had feelings for me. However, with Aman's confession, everything looked strangely out of control. Now, I was a part of a love triangle.

I knew I needed help to figure out the solution, so I thought of calling Samar. I had almost dialled his number when suddenly it crossed my mind that Samar had become possessive about me of late. He would freak out if I told him that someone has asked me out.

I took some deep breaths to declutter my mind. Soon, I came up with a solution. I knew what to do next.

9

The Dilemma

Ashna

I was sitting in Starbucks, sipping from my cup of hazelnut latte when my friend came in. I had ordered the grande cup as I knew I would need to get caffeinated to get through this.

'Hey,' said Maira. She rushed in and got seated.

'Now tell me what has happened? Why did you call me here so urgently?' she asked taking a sip of my latte.

'Mmm! This is good. Maybe I should order one for myself,' she said licking her lips.

'There is something I want you to know,' I said.

'Oh! Gossip?' she asked in sheer excitement.

'Something very weird happened with me,' I said. Then, after a pause I continued,' Let me be very clear, you need not worry because I am not going to do anything about it,' I said.

'Why should I worry about something that happened to you?' she asked, shrugging her shoulders casually.

'Okay, I don't know how to put this,' I paused for few seconds and said, 'Aman asked me out today.'

She looked shocked.

'What? Did he really ask you out, like really? He asked you out?' she asked, all in one single breath.

'Technically, yes. When our meeting got cancelled, Aman asked me to have lunch with him. Then, he offered to drop me to the nearest metro station and that's where he told me that he liked me,' I narrated everything.

'Wow! I had no clue that…,' she paused, looking directly at me, 'that he liked you.'

'I know! He has known me for mere two months. I never imagined that he would say something like this to me, Maira,' I said.

'Maybe,' she replied, clearly lost in her thoughts.

Her response testified the fact that she wasn't taking this whole thing very well. I sensed that it was the best time to reveal my plans to her.

'Maira, this was a big shock for me too, but I need your help. You must have thought of doing this anyway, but we don't have much time,' I said as if I was compelling her to take up a secret mission.

She nodded at me, hinting at me to continue.

'Tell Aman that you like him,' I blurted out.

At first, she seemed a little confused, but then, she seemed to have understood.

'Why would I do that?' she asked, clearly feigning innocence.

'Because you like Aman!' I said, exasperated at having to explain everything to her.

'I ... what?' she asked, almost jumping out of her seat.

'Don't act as if you don't know what I am talking about. I know you like Aman. And now is the time to confess your feelings to him. I have seen the chemistry between you both. It is important that you tell him; that way he will understand that he likes you and not me,' I said.

This was the plan that I had come up with while sitting at the metro station. However, it vanished in a jiffy as Maira burst out laughing.

'What did you say? Aman?' she asked in between her laughter. 'How did you even reach this conclusion?' she exclaimed.

'It's so evident. I have seen it as well. Remember, how he keeps calling you to his cabin, and you get offended whenever anybody calls him Hitler. Also, I've seen how you are always beaming with joy when he is around,' I replied confidently.

'That's it? On these small assumptions, you concluded that I like him? Ashna you are too funny,' she said.

'You don't?' I asked her, baffled at how stupid I had lately been behaving.

'Of course not! We are just acquaintances and nothing more than that. He calls me frequently to his cabin because I have been working in Biztech for a longer period as compared to you and Rajat. And I'll feel bad for anyone if people make fun of him behind his back. I don't understand how you can confuse basic courtesy with the feeling of love.' When she said this, I realized how pathetic I was at judging people and situations around me.

Looking at me so perplexed, Maira continued, 'Ashna, now when you know the truth, why don't you give your relationship a try?' she continued, looking at me.

'You can't be serious, Maira. You already know how messed up my life is. How can you even suggest this in spite of knowing everything about me and Samar?' I was bewildered at her suggestion.

'See, Aman is a nice guy. You know that, plus just think how good it can be for your career. In fact, it will be a great start for your career,' she said, winking at me.

'Shut up, I can't do this to Samar. I won't ever do anything that might hurt him,' I said, firm in my decision.

'Do you think you will help Samar this way? He won't move on ever. Till the time you are available, his hopes will never die. He will always think that someday you will fall in love with him. All you are doing right now is not letting him move forward in life. He deserves to move on to better things,' she said, in a grave tone.

'No, this isn't true. I can do anything for his happiness. I will always put him before me,' I replied confidently.

'Oh really? Then why don't you do what he wants? Why don't you get into a relationship with him? As far as I know, that's what he wants the most,' she asked looking at me questioningly, while sipping the last of my hazelnut latte.

I had no answer. Perhaps the conflict was more complex than I had perceived it to be.

10

More than Friends?

Samar

Moving steadily through the hills, surrounded by a picturesque sky which was touched by mountain ranges and serene meadow valleys full of beautiful step farms and small cottage houses, we reached Kausani at around 2.30 p.m.

It had taken almost twelve hours for us to reach there, but I wasn't complaining. The journey became memorable for me when Ashna placed her head on my shoulder and locked my arm in hers to take a nap.

As soon as we got down from the car, a cool and misty mountain breeze ruffled our hair and touched our cheeks, giving us a soothing sensation.

We installed our luggage at the guest house that Biztech had booked for her and rushed to freshen up. Then we left for our respective destinations. Ashna had informed me that her manager Aman had cancelled at the last moment as he had to go to attend some other meetings. Thus, she had to take charge and inspect the site on her own and file a report, which could take up a few hours. Now that she had to handle everything on her own, she wasn't afraid of making mistakes. In fact, she became confident. I didn't want to disturb her, so I decided to wander about Kasauni on my own.

I dropped Ashna at the site and requested the driver for a small city tour. However, due to time crunch, I could only visit the Baijnath temple. It was believed to be the place where lord Shiva had stayed with goddess Parvati after their marriage. Visiting that temple was a great experience because it rendered an unusual peace to my soul.

On my way back, I enquired with some locals about other places that we could visit at night because I knew that Ashna would take time. The locals told me that one of the main attractions of Kausani included the sight-seeing experience of a part of the Himalayan range. Also, there were few tea estates that had fresh tea plantations which had beautiful sunset and sunrise spots.

In spite of all these places, I wanted to plan something that could make that trip a memorable experience for Ashna.

I called up Ashna to tell her to be ready. I took her to one of the mountain roads where there were shops selling different varieties of tea, ranging from masala chai, ginger tea, lemon tea and many others.

'Where are we?' she asked me while stepping out of the car.

'Let's go and make this trip unforgettable,' I said and started moving ahead.

'But what are we doing here?' she continued to pester me with her questions.

'Follow my lead and you will get to know,' I replied, and moved across the road, holding Ashna's hand. We reached the the edge of a step farm, with lush green plantation that looked as fresh as morning dew.

'Tea estates?' she asked, turning towards me with a broad smile on her face.

I nodded at her and started walking upwards towards a small hilly path that was built for the tourists to help them navigate through different levels of the tea farm and enjoy the green view.

'You know Samar, I always wanted to visit Darjeeling because I wanted to see the tea gardens there,' she said excitedly.

The path was a little steep, slippery and muddy, but we didn't stop till we reached its highest point. I reached the top first, and then gave a hand to Ashna to pull her up comfortably. As she came up, she followed my gaze and exhaled with amazement. We were silent because we wanted to absorb the beauty of what lay in front of us. It was inexplicable.

Breathtakingly beautiful Himalayan range covered with fresh laden snow pierced through a translucent sheet of clouds, as if proclaiming their victory over them. They glowed with a crimson hue that the setting sun had imparted over them.

I could not help but wonder how it would feel to stand right at the centre of that range. It was a captivating view, and at its foot stood an equally mesmerizing valley, perhaps the greenest and freshest I had ever seen.

Little houses scattered throughout the valley gave out small streams of smoke that merged with the clouds. Everything looked so surreal!

When she saw me looking at her, she spoke with outstretched arms gesturing towards the view, 'I love it! This is the best thing I have ever set my eyes upon. Thank you so much Samar!'

'You don't need to thank me. There's more to come,' I replied with a wink.

'What can be better than this?' she asked, looking perplexed.

'Wait for some time. Everything will happen right here in front of us,' I said and we waited. She couldn't take her eyes off the view and I couldn't take my eyes off her. She seemed more beautiful. She had a naive smile on her face and her eyes sparkled with anticipation, waiting for what was to happen next.

Soon, the evening transformed into night and the mountains disappeared, paving way for the stars to take the limelight. I couldn't believe that a clear sky could harbour so many stars because Delhi's sky had never been this star-studded. Not just the sky, but the valley which had been lush green a few moments ago, now seemed like a sky on earth, housing thousands of stars. The light coming from the houses made it look magnificent.

'Samar, can you believe this, we are miles away from Delhi, sitting here atop this tea farm, witnessing this magical scene,' she spoke, breaking the reverie that we were a part of.

'Doesn't this feel like a verse out of a beautiful poem! All credit goes to you, Samar,' she exclaimed, with a mesmerized look on her face.

I realized how utterly romantic the scenario had turned out to be. I was there, sitting with the love of my life, witnessing a beautiful scene. I looked at her face again, and she noticed and smiled at me. We looked at each other for a few seconds. I noticed her gleaming eyes, her tender cheeks that I wanted to touch, her hair that I wanted to caress and her lips that I wanted to kiss.

We were looking at each other when impulsively I took her face in my hands, and softly brushed her cheeks. I leaned in and kissed her with all my heart, pouring out the emotions I had been holding in forever. She didn't object and kissed me back, sealing our first ever kiss. It satisfied every bit of my soul. I couldn't think anything for that moment. It was surreal.

As we drew apart, she opened her eyes. Perhaps, she was as surprised as I was.

When I looked up at her, she was looking down towards the valley. I couldn't dare to say anything to her. All I had ever wanted was for her to reciprocate my feelings.

Finally, it had happened.

❖

Ashna

We sat atop a tea farm and the most beautiful face of nature lay in front of us. I had never seen something so amazing in my entire life. Everything seemed magical. I felt as if I was floating in the air of serenity that surrounded us. I wanted to thank Samar for making this moment happen; it was so perfect.

I turned towards him to say something, but he was already looking at me. I noticed sheer happiness on his face. Maybe that moment's magic had cast a spell on him too.

We looked at each other for a few seconds. I started to speak, but before I could, he suddenly leaned in towards me and kissed me. It was difficult to process. However, I didn't push him away, not because I wanted the kiss, but only because Samar wasn't any random guy. He was my friend, my support system. How could I have hurt him? How could I have told him that I didn't want it!

I had celebrated the fact that Aman had cancelled at the last moment. But, never in my wildest dream could I have imagined that something like this could happen between me and Samar.

Why did Samar kiss me? I thought he had moved on, then why did he do it? All this time, I had been ignoring Samar's behaviour, but I understood that he had never moved on. Why did I become destiny's favourite toy?

I knew that I had given him a wrong indication by not objecting to the kiss. He could be led to think that I too loved him. But, I didn't.

Maira's words started to echo in my head. Whatever she had said a few days ago about Samar seemed true. It was true that I was the reason he wasn't moving on. I had clung to him and wasn't letting him go.

We went down the tea farm almost an hour after the kiss. Silence pervaded between us. On our way back, I avoided any conversation about the kiss. Samar put my head on his shoulder whenever he would see that I wasn't sleeping comfortably or that I woke up by a jerk.

However, to me, even this friendly gesture seemed strange. I didn't like that sudden change in our chemistry. I was determined to clear the air between us even though the stakes were high.

11

The Unsettling Truth

Samar

When someone loves you unconditionally, the world around you seems more beautiful than before. Days are happier. The moon shines brighter. The flowers seem to bloom earlier, and everything looks perfect. Straight out of a fairy tale!

After that moment at Kausani, I too felt the same. All of a sudden, all the cliché rom-com shows got me interested. All romantic songs started playing inside my head. I started smiling more. I began to wonder why I had changed so much. It was strange and yet, I loved it.

Even though Ashna had not objected to our kiss, she had not said anything to me thereafter. I wanted to hear from her that she loved me. I knew that after the kiss, these expressions would be mere formality, but still it seemed important to me. That is why I decided to ask her out again.

Kartik had invited us to his house for his parents' twenty-fifth anniversary. At first, I wasn't willing to go there as it was a small affair with close family. But then, he told me that he had invited us over so that I could spend time with Ashna and get to know about her feelings. He had instructed me to keep my proposal simple this time.

Kartik's parents greeted me very warmly as I handed them a bouquet of carnations and orchids I had picked up on the way. I found Kartik near the kitchen, pouring soft-drink in disposable glasses.

'Hey, do you need any help?' I asked him, moving forward to our classic handshake.

'Hey, you came,' he said, moving forward. "Great! Hold this and help me,' he said, signalling towards the glass. I did as he instructed.

While helping him, I asked, 'By the way, is Ashna here yet?' I asked in between.

'Yes, she's inside with two of my cousins. She came half an hour earlier so I asked two of my sisters to give her company. Now go find her and talk to her. Actually, don't talk to her anything about you guys here. Talk about it when you walk her home,' he said, as if he had already put in a lot of thought into this for us.

'Walk her home?' I said, my eyes glaring at him in disbelief.

'Yes Samar, you will walk her home and then talk about your feelings, because nothing can be better than a romantic walk at night. Haven't you seen any good romantic movies? This idea never fails,' he said, looking at me.

'Sounds like a plan,' I replied, smiling back at him.

I peeked into the room where Ashna was. She was talking to the two girls. She was dressed in an impeccable black *churidaar* suit, with a small black *bindi.* When I saw her, she was tucking away a strand of her hair behind her ear.

She noticed me and I waved at her. She smiled back at me.

We sat together for dinner. I noticed that Ashna had been very quiet throughout the party. More so, she hadn't spoken to me ever since we were back from the trip. I had called her several times, but whenever I did, she had either been busy with office work, or was too tired to talk.

Once we were done with the dinner and it was time to leave, Kartik suggested that it was late and that I should walk Ashna home. She objected to it instantly. However, we didn't budge from our plan and she caved in at last. Kartik looked at me and his expression was clear – he had done his work and I had to do mine.

It was around 10 p.m. and the bustle of the Delhi streets had somewhat subsided. The roads were not completely empty, but had fewer people than usual. I was walking with my hands in my pocket and she was walking beside me. None of us spoke for a long time. Her silence had started to bother me as I was unable to understand the reason behind it.

It could be that she wanted to redefine our relationship after the kiss. I wanted to be the best friend who became her boyfriend, not the boyfriend who was once her best friend. Because, no matter what, I wanted to be the guy with whom she could be honest about her feelings. Her silence was overbearing and instead of drawing assumptions, I sought answers.

'Ashna, what happened?' I said and gave her a playful shoulder tug. She smiled but didn't say anything.

'Don't just smile, tell me what has happened to you?

'Nothing,' she said in a low voice and kept walking. I stopped in between, and since she had walked a few steps ahead, she stopped and turned back.

'Are you telling me or not?' I asked, keeping a calm but serious expression on my face. 'You and I both know that there is something that is bothering you and I won't move forward unless you tell me what it is,' I said, standing adamantly on the road.

She kept quiet for few more seconds and then she finally began. 'Yes, I do need to tell you something,' she said, without looking me in the eye.

I felt happy. Finally Ashna was about to express herself to me. I could feel a sudden rush of excitement in my veins.

'What?' I asked with apparent happiness.

'First, you have to promise me that no matter what, nothing will change between us,' she said.

Now, more than ever, I was sure that I was right. Ashna was just worried about how the change in our relationship status would affect our friendship. However, before I could tell her that there was nothing to worry about, I noticed that her face had turned red and tears were rolling down her cheeks.

'Nothing will ever change between us, I promise you,' I said, making another promise, one that I wanted to keep forever.

'Samar, I have gotten into a committed relationship with someone in my office,' she said, her head hung low as she spoke to the ground.

I looked at her in disbelief. For a few seconds, I just couldn't gather what she meant by a committed relationship.

Her words pierced through my heart. I couldn't speak. I couldn't even blink my eyes. It was as if my senses had stopped functioning and a hollow emptiness was taking over my body. I remained still for a while, allowing her words to sink into my psyche.

'Rajat?' I asked with a heavy voice.

'No, it's Aman,' she said, wiping off her nose and making a sniffing sound.

This was the final blow. I had no idea that Aman was anywhere in the picture. He was just her manager. I felt dejected at the fact that she chose a stranger over me, her best friend

'Do you love him?' I mustered the courage to ask this pertinent question, unable to control my tears.

'He asked me out, and he is a nice guy. I don't really know anything about love, but this will help you move on, Samar. Please move on,' she said pleadingly.

What? You did this for my sake? Thank you so much. You have done me a big favour. You will be doing me a favour every time you'll kiss him or touch him. These thoughts were racing in my head. I wanted to blurt them out, but I couldn't.

'Samar, you were not moving on. You became very possessive. And at Kausani, you even let your feelings overrule your senses. That's why I had to do this. I think this will be good for both of us,' she said, breaking my heart into innumerable pieces even further.

I hated myself for kissing her. All this while, I believed that it had been mutual, but it was not. I felt like a molester when she said that I had let my feelings overrule my senses. The best night of my life had turned into a nightmare. Tears welled up in my eyes, and I was about to break down, when I swallowed my pain.

'You didn't even give me a chance, Ashna. Anyway, congratulations!' I said and turned around to leave. There was nothing left to say. I had lost everything. Few shattered pieces of our memories remained, but I didn't want to carry them forward with me.

Ashna came running behind me and turned me around to hug me tightly. Not a side hug, but a warm hug, the one that I had longed for since forever. It was our first hug, but I had never imagined that it would happen under such circumstances.

'Samar, you promised me that nothing would change between us,' she said slowly, looking deep into my eyes.

I nodded. But I knew that everything was over between us. We were not best friends anymore. I didn't want to be a part of her life, because obviously, I wasn't good enough for her.

I used to believe that I was the hero of our story, but she never perceived me as *her* hero. This bitter truth had changed everything between us.

❖

Failed and frustrated, I reached home. I had cried my heart out on my way back. The only thing I had ever wanted was snatched away from me. I wiped off my tears before entering home. Then, I went straight to Divish.

'I want that job. Is the offer still up?' I asked him.

He muted the television and looked at me, very surprised at my demeanour.

'Did something happen?' he enquired in a concerned tone.

'No,' I replied trying to sound casual, even though I was broken from inside. 'I just realized that all my friends are working and I can't just sit at home and wait for my cartoons to get published. I'd rather take that job,' I said. In reality, I wanted to distract my mind away from Ashna. Finally, I wanted to get over her.

'Okay, but that job is gone. I told you to appear, but you didn't, so they hired someone else,' he said.

'Is there any other job? Anything would do, even if it's outside Delhi,' I asked, helplessly cursing my fate.

'There are some openings in Mumbai, but they are neither related to architecture nor cartooning. They are very basic jobs, and I'm sure you wouldn't want to move to Mumbai for that,' he said, his tone changing to an enquiring one.

'No issues! I don't have any problem with moving to Mumbai. It would be good exposure. You just have to make sure I get it,' I responded shortly.

How will you manage in Mumbai?' he asked.

'I will manage. You must help me to get the job,' I replied.

'Getting it won't be a problem, but will you be happy doing it?' he said slowly.

'It doesn't matter anymore.'

12

Taking the Next Step

Few months later

Ashna

It was a hectic day again. Ever since the Kausani project had been approved, Biztech had become much more stressful than before. I had to work extra shifts and yet I was always surrounded by blueprints and designs, even at home.

'Don't take so much stress, Ashna. I will help you to finalize the design,' said Aman as he gave me a peck on my cheek right before I got out of his car. He had come to drop me home like every day. It had been almost three months and our relationship was going strong.

'I know you will help me figure it out,' I said smilingly as I waved him a goodbye.

He drove away while I turned to walk towards my house. I couldn't help but wonder how Aman was just perfect for me. He was exactly the kind of guy I wanted. He was successful, supportive, understanding and of course, handsome. Most importantly, he respected my boundaries and never tried to force his opinions on me. What made him different than the others was the fact that he never tried to make any sexual advances towards me, even after three months of our relationship. So, I guess I was happy with him.

But in spite of that, I was still unclear about the notion of love. Reality is very different from how we perceive love to be. Violins don't play in the background, the wind doesn't blow your hair lightly and leaves don't drop from the trees in slow motion. Nothing of this cinematic drama happens. Everything remains as it is, except for the fact that you tend to feel special in the company of your partner.

Circumstances played an important role in love, in bringing us closer, because he was the only person in my life whom I could call my friend. All the other people who were once close to me had moved far away from my life.

Sakshi was still in Bengaluru and we hardly spoke. Maira had also left Biztech to move to Pune to pursue some film-making course. Sakshi and Maira were both important to me and I cared for them, but not as much as I did for Samar.

It was midnight and all the designs and blueprints that needed to be worked on were spread on my study table. I sat by the window of my room, scrolling through the memories which I had once captured in my phone.

The impact of photographs is very strange as they have the power to transport us into the past. They take you to your cherished memories, the people you had once loved, even though they are not a part of your present.

I was cherishing my memories with Samar from the time when we were together and happy. I would often look at our old photographs, reminiscing the good time that we had spent together. It had become a routine for me.

I often wondered how nothing would have changed if I had not felt that he was becoming over-possessive. Or if that kiss wouldn't have happened. These two events changed the course of our connection.

Was it fair for Samar to have abandoned me? Couldn't we have talked it out and overcome this rough patch together? Was our bond that weak?

He neither gave me a chance to explain myself, nor did he understand that whatever I did was to protect our friendship. I contacted Kartik to enquire about him, but it was too late. He told me that Samar had moved to Mumbai for a job.

I felt an excruciating pain when I heard this. It was hurtful to realize that once we were most significant to each other, only to end up being strangers.

Convincing myself that whatever I did was right, I plugged my phone into the charger and got into bed to get some sleep. Before I could, my phone beeped. The messages were from Aman, and who else could have messaged me apart from him. Since I was not asleep, I thought it fit to talk to him.

Aman
Hey! Awake?
Ashna
Hey yes.

Aman

I hope you were not asleep.

Ashna

No, I was just about to.

Aman

Good then I messaged right on time. So what's up? What were you doing?

Ashna

Nothing much, just trying to come up with a few designs.

I couldn't tell him that I had been thinking about Samar and that I was missing him. In fact, I had not told him anything about Samar.

I knew that Aman was mature enough to understand the bond that Samar and I had, but still, I wasn't comfortable in sharing about my personal life with him, even though he was my boyfriend.

Perhaps the major reason behind my hesitation was that I had always shared my thoughts with Samar. We connected so well that I could express my thoughts freely and unapologetically, without being judged.

I believed that only Samar could understand me completely, which is why my heart couldn't replace him with anybody else. However, Samar was my best friend. There is always a thin line between friendship and a romantic relationship. I did not want to blur the distinction.

Aman

I told you to not worry about them. We will manage to come up with some ideas tomorrow.

Ashna

I know, but I wanted to put some effort into it and come up with something on my own.

Aman

Okay, if that's your wish. It will be great if you can come up with something on your own. Anyway, I don't want to discuss work, I want to talk about something related to us.

Ashna

Okay, what is it?

Aman

See, it's been three months since we have been together, but don't you think that our relationship is heading nowhere? I mean, I like to spend time with you and I am sure you do too, but don't you think that we are still at the same place where we were three months ago?

Ashna

I am sorry, but I don't think I understand what you are trying to say.

Aman

I am trying to say that I think it's time to for us to take our relationship a step further.

What does he really mean by a step further? Does he want to get intimate with me? Did I think of him as a nice guy too soon?

Ashna

Step further? I still didn't get you.

Aman

It's simple Ashna; I want you to meet my friends. I have already told them about you and they are super excited to see you.

I sighed with relief as I read his message. *Thank god it wasn't about sex.*

I clearly needed more time before I could be intimate with him.

Ashna

Sure, I would love to meet them. When is the plan?

Aman

Great! We are meeting next week, would you come along?

Ashna

Do you think it would be appropriate for me to join you people? Won't it look awkward that suddenly I am tagging along with you?

Aman

Don't worry, they are cool with it and it is totally appropriate ☺

Ashna

Then it's fine.

Aman

Cool, I will pick you up. And one more thing, I wanted to tell you something very important. I will tell you once you have met my friends.

What was Aman talking about? What was he up to?

I could only wonder.

13

Breaking Out of my Comfort Zone

Samar

How to find new friends?
Communities for singles in Mumbai.
People looking for friends in Mumbai.
How to make your social life more interesting?
New apps to make friends.

These were some topics I had recently searched on Google. Finally, after almost three months, I was certain that I was ready to make new friends in Mumbai.

Kartik hadn't agreed with my decision when I told him that I was moving to Mumbai. He felt that I was over-reacting and that I had taken this decision because I was overwhelmed with emotions. He was right. I was heartbroken, defeated and full of despair. I didn't have the courage to face Ashna again. I couldn't bear to see her happy in a relationship with someone else.

I decided to move to Mumbai because the city held a different meaning for everyone. For some, it was about hope that prevailed in every nook and corner of this city. For some, it was a city of dreams. However, for me, this city was a healer. It had strengthened me from within.

I felt as if I had just suffered a break-up. I would sulk around all day, trying to figure out what I lacked because of which Ashna couldn't love me. I would think deeply and try to come up with reasons why we were not together. I earnestly waited for the day when she would realize that her relationship with Aman was a big mistake.

Sometimes, I unblocked her from WhatsApp and Facebook to check if she was happy. Her smiling pictures soothed my pain. But whenever I found her pictures with Aman, my heart would be filled with agony and grief. Which is when this city helped me regain my self-confidence. I travelled in the local trains and walked besides the Marine Drive, watching the magnificent necklace formation. I visited the Siddhi Vinayak temple and Haji Ali, finding solace. I walked barefoot on the beaches of Versova and Juhu where the water softly touched my feet, taking away all my worries and pains with it. The soothing sound of the waves hitting the rocks, amidst the hustle-bustle of the vibrant city worked like music to my soul.

Soon, my feelings for Ashna seemed to wither away and I started to realize that I had been wrong all these years. I had always believed that what I felt for Ashna was love, but it never was. It had always been infatuation. Maybe it was an obsession that I had developed over time. I always kept trying to make her fall in love with me, not realizing that true love can never be enforced. It stems from within.

Even though my self-esteem was improving, I was not happy with my job. I was only grateful that it had given me an opportunity to live in Mumbai. I knew that cartooning was my passion and I wanted to pursue it.

I had already submitted some of my cartoons and illustrations to some magazines in Delhi and Mumbai, adhering to their respective styles and types. But, they got rejected which was very puzzling to me. However, that didn't deter me, because I knew success never came easy. I had nurtured this dream for so long, and now I was ready to strive for it.

Since my professional life was somewhat sorted, I still had to build my personal life. I had no friends in Mumbai. Since I had moved on from Ashna, I felt the need to meet new people. It was a sudden energy that had bloomed inside me, encouraging me to break out of my comfort zone.

I finally found a way to meet new people. Tinder!

I had heard about Tinder at my office when two of my desperately single colleagues were talking about it.

I searched about it on Google and found out that it was a dating app that had come across as a boon for people like me, who were not very comfortable with talking to ladies, leave aside making any moves on them.

Excited to see what it was, I downloaded the app and created an account. I created my profile and put some of my best pictures on display. As soon as I got hold of some profiles, I started swiping right, without even looking at the pictures. Soon I ran out of likes and I had to wait for a match.

The most difficult aspect of this app was the phase of endless anticipation. I didn't have any matches till the next morning, which was concerning me.

Was I really not good enough for people who didn't even know me? If Ashna didn't find me suitable, then who else would? I thought, sighing with a heavy heart. I decided to uninstall Tinder. However, before I could, my notification bar glittered. 'Ping! You have a match.'

Without even bothering who the match was, I typed in 'hi' in the chat box. I was waiting for a reply, when I decided to check out her profile.

FilmyGirl? What sort of a name was that?

I surfed through her pictures to check the authenticity of her profile. She was wearing sunglasses in all her pictures. Soon she responded to my 'hi'.

FilmyGirl

Samar? Are you in Mumbai?

Samar

Yes, I am in Mumbai, what about you?

FilmyGirl

I too am in Mumbai, but when did you come here. I mean are you here for work or are you visiting someone?'

Samar
No offence, but how did you know that I have moved to Mumbai. Isn't it possible that I was already living here?
FilmyGirl
Samar, you are kidding, right?
Samar
No, I am really curious. Because as far as I know, we are talking for the first time and we don't know each other. How did you manage to guess that I had moved to Mumbai?
FilmyGirl
What? That's because I already know that you belong from Delhi.

I was stunned. I had not mentioned anywhere in my profile that I belonged to Delhi.

Samar
This is scary. How do you know that I am from Delhi?'
FilmyGirl
Oh, I thought you were kidding, but you really haven't recognized me. Samar, I know this because we already know each other and this is certainly not the first time we are talking.
Samar
We know each other? I think you are mistaken. I don't know many people in Mumbai. You seem so beautiful. If I would have known you, I wouldn't have forgotten.
FilmyGirl
Firstly, thank you for the indirect compliment, and secondly, I am not from Mumbai. We know each other from Delhi. I am Maira, Ashna's friend. We met at Cheeros, remember?
Samar
Maira? Wow! Are you serious?
FilmyGirl
Haha, of course I am Maira. Do you have any doubt?

Samar
Yes, in all your pictures, you don't look like the person I met at Cheeros.
FilmyGirl
Haha, because when we met that day, I was dressed in formals. Maybe that's why you didn't recognise me.
Samar
I still can't believe that you are Maira. Wow, what are the odds that we both were in Mumbai and we met through Tinder?
Maira
That's hilarious, isn't it?
Samar
It is for sure. So, what are you doing in Mumbai?
Maira
I would like to answer this only when we meet for coffee or something. Let's meet up.

I wasn't sure, because it's true that I wanted to meet someone, but I didn't know whether I should have accepted Maira's offer. After all, she was Ashna's friend and I was already running away from Ashna. It didn't seem like the right thing to do.

Samar
I don't know whether it would be a good idea.
Maira
It will be. You have to meet me Samar. I am already going crazy in Mumbai because I don't have any friends here. That's the reason why I took to Tinder to find new people. And look, I found you.

I was surprised at the unexpected turn of events. I decided to go with the flow. I was sure we could handle what happened from here.

'Let's meet,' I typed and sent it to her.

14

Commitment Phobia

Ashna

'This is what the hotel will look like,' announced Aman, pointing towards a blueprint that was neatly pinned on a table in front of us.

He continued, 'Ashna, I would like to thank you on behalf of our entire team for bringing up this design,' and everyone turned towards me.

I nodded in gratitude. I had finally come up with a design for the hotel at Kasauni which was well received. Aman, on the other hand, was being utterly modest because I hadn't done it on my own. He had helped me a lot in the process.

'So guys, let's get rolling! The design is ready and we will have to work really hard on this from tomorrow, so be prepared,' he said as the team ended up laughing and started to move out of the conference room.

'Ashna!' Aman called out to me and gestured me to wait.

'You did a great job,' he said, holding both my hands in his, as soon as all the people had left.

'Why did you give all the credit to me? I couldn't have completed the design without you,' I said, feeling thankful.

'You deserve it. You have really worked hard for this project,' he said and I smiled back at him, humbly. He continued, 'I love your enthusiasm and your hunger to thrive in your work,' he said, caressing my hands for a few seconds. I started to blush. However, we soon realized that we were in the office and had to maintain decorum.

He continued, 'By the way, I hope you remember that we have to go for dinner with my friends tonight,' he said.

'Yes, I remember and I have informed my parents that I'll be a little late,' I said reassuring him that I had not forgotten about it.

'Good, so shall we leave now?' he asked and I nodded.

We walked to the parking lot and I waited for him to bring out his car. To my surprise, Aman came out on a bike, followed by a thundering sound. He stopped right in front of me and removed his helmet.

'Hop on!' he said.

'Bike? What happened to your car?' I asked, while sitting behind him.

'My sister took the car in the morning. She always does this. Anyway, instead of calling her, I decided to take the bike. Also, it's way more romantic than a car,' he said, completing his sentence with a giggle.

'Fine,' I replied, chuckling and blushing as well.

'What?' I shouted through the helmet.

'You will have to hold me tight,' he said shouting back, and I blushed again.

Aman knew subtle ways of being romantic. I, on the other hand, was reluctant to hold him. Maybe because he was my boss. However, now he was perhaps the love of my life, so I needed to overcome this awkwardness and learn to reciprocate.

Hesitatingly, I put one hand on his shoulder and the other slightly around his waist. Suddenly, he accelerated the bike, which gave me a jerk and made me hug him tighter. He had pulled the classic tactic to bring me closer to him. I took advantage of the moment and pressed my cheek against his back with my eyes closed. I concentrated on his heartbeat, trying to feel them. However, even after few minutes, I couldn't feel any spark. Maybe it really was our professional relationship coming in the way of my feelings for him.

'This is the most romantic ride we have ever taken. I think I should be thankful to Mandaar for inviting us,' said Aman, bringing me out of my thoughts. I was still pressed against his back when suddenly it struck me that he had not yet told me why his friends had invited us for dinner. I mean he didn't tell me whether it was just a casual outing or something in particular.

I gestured Aman to slow down and then I asked, 'Do you people meet often?'

'No, we don't meet often. We all are busy and we hardly get time to meet each other, so we only meet on special occasions,' he said casually.

Are they really meeting for me? Am I the occasion for them? I thought.

'What's the occasion today?' I asked, just to be sure.

'It's Mandaar's birthday,' he said.

Phew! So at least it's not my muh-dikhaai. Wait! Is it a birthday party? I didn't buy any gift, my mind was racing, making me nervous.

'It's someone's birthday? You should have told me beforehand, at least I would have brought a gift for him. Now it will seem as if I am gate crashing his party,' I said, clearly disappointed.

'I have already bought something for him from your side. We just have to pick it up from a gift shop on our way,' he said, leaving me amazed at how considerate he was.

'Thank you so much,' I said looking admiringly at him. He gradually increased the speed, and on a clear night, beneath the open sky, when the cool wind touched my face, I knew that I had been wrong to doubt the idea of loving him.

We stopped at a gift store a few kilometres away from our office. He picked up Mandaar's gift, which was wrapped in a pretty box.

We walked up to Aman's bike which was parked in a by lane to the right of the gift shop. It was 9 p.m. already and the shop was isolated.

'Ashna,' said Aman, turning towards me, while I was waiting for him to start the bike.

'Yes?' I said, looking up to face him.

'I know it's only been three months since we're dating, but I never really got a chance to propose to you. I wanted to, but before I could plan anything, you said yes to me. Anyway, since now I can't really propose to you again, I just wanted to give you something,' he said, forwarding me Mandaar's gift.

'This? Didn't you pick this up for Mandaar?' I asked him, taking the box reluctantly.

'No,' he said, taking out another box from his pocket. 'This is for Mandaar. I had already picked this up in the morning. And we came here to pick this up,' he said, gesturing towards the box in my hand.

'Aman, there was no need for a gift,' I said. I somehow wasn't much excited about it.

'Open it,' he insisted.

I unwrapped the gift carefully. It was a black wooden box, just of the size of my palm. For once, I thought that he had bought me a watch. To my surprise, when I opened the box, I froze to my spot. My eyes were fixated on a glittering silver ring, an eternity ring bejewelled with some blue stones.

Was he already proposing for marriage? I was not ready for it. I couldn't marry him, I thought, silently freaking out in my head.

'Umm, Aman, a ring is given during a marriage proposal, so are you proposing?' I asked him, my voice was barely audible.

'No, don't get me wrong, this is not a marriage proposal ring,' he interrupted before I could complete my sentence. 'It's an eternity ring which symbolizes everlasting love between partners. So I thought of making an eternal promise of love to you,' he said, blushing to the extent that he couldn't even look at me directly.

He gathered some courage and continued, 'Plus, this is just a platinum plated ring with artificial stones, kind of temporary because I will replace it with a real platinum ring when I will truly ask you out for marriage,' he completed with a spark in his eyes.

I didn't know how to respond to that. I wasn't sure whether to accept the ring or not. The idea of an engagement gave me jitters. I know I had already accepted this relationship, but this was scary. The only thing was that I didn't know why I was getting cold feet.

'Ashna,' he said slowly, stepping a little closer to me. 'Look at the inner edge of the ring,' he demonstrated.

I took out the ring from the box and studied what was engraved on its inside edges. I had to use my phone's flash to see what it was. It read, *the meaning of love for me is you.*

He looked directly into my eyes and said, 'I got this engraved because it's true and I want you to remember it always,' he slowly took my left hand into his and put the ring on my index finger.

I was relieved to see that he didn't slip the ring on my third finger. I wasn't ready for that kind of a commitment. However, as soon as the ring became a part of me, it felt strange. I felt as if I couldn't breathe properly.

Why am I feeling like this? Is this the feeling of love, or is this happening because I am committing fully into this relationship by accepting this ring? Why does commitment scare me? I think I was clear that I loved Aman and there is no doubt that he loves me. Maybe I am panicking because my life is changing?'

The next moment, Aman was leaning in towards me. My mind was busy contemplating what he was about to do. I had two choices, either I could dodge him, or I could get carried away in the moment.

I too leaned in towards him with almost the same intensity, and we kissed. I had let myself free for the very first time after we had committed. I wanted to see how I felt about it.

Our kiss lasted a few seconds and when we were done, we both stood looking at each other. I saw a spark of joy and contentment in Aman's eyes. I understood that he had loved the introduction of this physical element into our relationship. Perhaps, now he won't feel that our relationship was going nowhere. However, I was unsure whether I was sailing in the same boat.

'Umm, let's go,' he said without making any eye contact with me. I didn't nod or say anything.

As we drove through the night, I closed my eyes, trying to rewind the kiss with Aman. I wanted to recollect my thoughts from that moment. It was hard to do so because every time I tried to think about it, my mind wandered off to the breathtaking hills of Kausani, where Samar had kissed me.

I soon realized that as soon as our lips had met, Samar was revolving in my head. Maybe because before this, the last kiss I had was with him.

Samar was my best friend, but just a friend. Kissing him had been a mistake, but kissing Aman was not. How could I even compare them? Why am I thinking about Samar when I should be thinking about Aman? Why am I so confused all the time? Why are these thoughts coming to my mind? I wondered. I was tired of being confused all the time.

'Ashna,' shouted Aman, breaking away my imaginary courtroom drama where I stood in the witness box probing myself.

'Yes?' I shouted back, because we were still driving.

'Remember, I wanted to tell you something after you had met my friends?' he shouted back.

'Yes! Obviously, that has been bothering me since the last week. I didn't mention it because I thought you would tell me yourself whenever you wanted to,' I replied.

'I feel that this is the right time to tell you,' he continued.

'Okay, I'm listening,' I replied.

'Don't freak out because there are chances that you might,' he said and I laughed.

'You don't worry, because I am used to getting freaked out every now and then,' I said.

He turned his face slightly towards the left and removed the glass lid of his helmet, so that I could hear him properly as he continued to drive. 'Actually, what I need to tell you—'

Crash!

We collided with something, because for a second, he had diverted his attention from the road. Before I could react, our bike was down and I was sliding across the rugged concrete. Everything happened in a jiffy.

A moment later, I lay in the middle of the road surrounded by some unknown faces. I was conscious so I looked around for Aman. I saw him getting up at a distance, and he was running towards me. I was satisfied that he was fine. I tried to get up, but a severe pain caught my leg. Everything went hazy before I blacked out.

15

Meeting a New Friend

Samar

Maira and I had agreed to meet at Cafe Mondegar in Colaba. It was one of the oldest cafés in the city and I had heard a lot about it.

I was nervous to see her because I had never interacted much with other girls, apart from Ashna. Even though Maira and I used to talk through messages, I was still worried about presenting myself in front of her during our meeting.

While travelling from Church Gate station to Colaba in the auto, all I thought of was how I should behave in front of her. Somewhere at the back of my mind, I was trying to accept the fact that by meeting her, I was allowing Ashna back in my life, even if it was in an indirect manner. I didn't know whether I was ready for it.

It was easy to spot Cafe Mondegar because it was situated on the main road in the Metro House building, Colaba. I decided to text Maira to check where she was.

Samar
Hey Maira, I have reached Mondegar, where are you?
Maira
Hey! Just come inside. I already got a table for us.

As I stepped inside, I was fascinated by the ambience of the café. It was modern, yet it had a subtle vintage feel to it. The tables were placed closer to each other in comparison to regular cafes and all of them had a pink and white chequered table cloth. However, what captivated me the most was the intricate cartooning on its walls. From a loving couple with hearts all around them to a goofy-faced person enjoying a bite, the wall was filled with interesting illustrations and caricatures.

I looked around for Maira, but I couldn't find her. Suddenly, I saw an elegant girl dressed in a yellow *kurti* and red *patiala* salwar which was paired with silver jhumkas. Her hair was long and wavy and that small yellow *bindi* shining right at the centre of her forehead looked adorable.

'Maira?' I asked, walking towards her.

'Yes, of course. I am Maira,' she said, smiling at me as she stretched out a hand for a handshake. It was then when I noticed her blue-green eyes, which had enchanted me when we had met at Cheeros in Delhi.

'I didn't recognize you at all. How do you manage to look so different all the time?' I shook her hand while asking this question. From a trendy professional look to a graceful

Indian traditional look, she was definitely very versatile when it came to fashion.

'Haha! You're just generous with compliments. Anyway, are you always this modest or am I really special?' she replied in her pleasant voice.

'I guess you are very special,' I replied, smiling back at her.

'Wow, thank you so much. I am flattered. By the way, we have met for the first time, and—'

'Second,' I interrupted, 'Sorry, carry on,' I said, smiling pleasantly.

'Oh! And you have already started flirting with me,' she giggled.

'Flirting? No, I am not flirting with you. It was just surprising to see how perfectly you always carry yourself. That's why I said it,' I defended.

'Samar,' she said in a serious tone, 'I am just kidding!' She said and giggled.

'So tell me, what brought you to Mumbai?' she asked inquisitively.

'I am here for a job,' I replied, rather nervously.

'Okay, where do you work?' she continued interrogating me like an officer.

'I am into the operations department of a medicine startup Med-a-Door. What about you? Are you here on a vacation?' I asked her, wondering what she was doing in Mumbai when she had a job in Delhi.

'No, I am not on a vacation. I left Biztech. I am here to pursue a certificate course in Film-making. Originally, it was in Pune, but then they shifted our classes to their Mumbai campus, so I came here. I know this might sound absurd that I left a stable job at Biztech to pursue something like film-making that does not even guarantee an income, but I wanted to dedicate myself to my passion,' she said, shrugging her shoulders.

'This doesn't sound absurd at all. In fact, to me it sounds sensible because I am also looking for a way out of my job. I want to pursue a career in cartooning and I am desperately in search of an opportunity to begin my journey. I have even submitted my cartoons to various newspaper and magazine publishers, but till now I haven't received any positive response from them. I am hopeful that one day I will eventually come up with something which will get published,' I said, with a sense of pride and confidence.

'Wow, cartooning seems different and exciting. We are so much alike. I am glad we met. You must really love this café then?' she asked pointing towards the cartoons on the wall.

'I totally love it. I was thinking how alike we are. I guess, all creative people are similar when it comes to their passion towards their craft,' I said while she nodded in agreement.

After talking for a while, we decided to place our order. She ordered a fresh pineapple juice along with vegetarian bruschetta and I ordered an espresso with a grilled sandwich.

We talked a bit more about Mumbai and shared some of our personal experiences. We were so engrossed in talking that we didn't realize how an entire hour passed away.

When our food arrived, I immediately gorged on my sandwich. While we were eating, she said, 'Samar, I guess now we are friends, right?'

'Of course, we are friends,' I replied with a smile.

I was already considering her a friend, which is why I was compelled to share my story with her.

'I really longed to have a friend in Mumbai,' she said smiling at me.

I felt happy because I wanted the same too.

We talked about random things at first, before she steered the conversation towards Ashna. I was reluctant to tell her the truth at first, but also knew that I needed to vent it out. Contemplating what all I could tell her, I started stirring my cup of espresso. Then I got lost in my reverie.

'And this brings us right here, at this café,' I completed narrating my story to Maira, heaving a sigh of relief.

Maira kept staring at me without uttering a word. After almost two-and-a-half hours of speaking continuously, amidst three cups of espressos, three glasses of juice, one bruschetta, one grilled sandwich and two pasta dishes, I had narrated my entire story to her.

At first, it was difficult to relive all those moments as the sorrow of losing Ashna would surge up to my heart and sting me intensely. However, Maira's touch and compassion had made this process very effortless and liberating.

Even though she was aware of Ashna's point of view in our story, she was able to understand my pain. I was happy and relieved that I had shared it with her. I needed someone's comforting presence to vent out all my feelings and heal.

'I understand your feelings, Samar. Because you loved someone purely, but didn't get the love you deserved. Nothing can hurt more than this,' she spoke at last.

'I know that you understood a part of my feelings, but you cannot understand it fully. No one can, except the one who has felt this pain,' I replied.

'Maybe you are right, but tell me one thing, are you not going to talk to her ever?' she asked.

'I won't. I don't want to feel that pain again,' I replied, pretty sure of what I wanted.

'But, doesn't love mean to let go? Doesn't it mean that you let the person you love find their happiness? Samar, in your case, Ashna was not just someone you loved; she was your best friend. Won't you forgive her?' she asked expectantly.

I knew that Maira had a point, but she could never comprehend the pain I felt on being turned down by someone who was most dear to me. She chose a stranger over me, which was the most heartbreaking experience of my life. I could never forgive her. For me, her decision would always be selfish.

'I don't know what love means. I have never experienced it, but I don't think I will ever be able to forgive Ashna because what she did was selfish,' I replied bluntly.

'Okay, that's your personal decision. But I thought that after her accident, you might forgive her. But since you don't want to so—'

'Wait, what? Accident? Whose accident?' I jumped up, interrupting her.

'Ashna met with an accident. Don't you know?' she asked me, looking surprised.

'What accident?' I was shocked.

'Yes, she was in a road accident a few days ago. She fell off a bike and got injured. Luckily, she is fine. I thought you already knew about it,' she said, leaving me stunned.

My throat went dry. I could feel chilling vibrations throughout my body. I looked at Maira, but couldn't speak. It felt as if I was paralyzed for a few seconds.

How could she be hurt? Whose bike was that? How is she? Did something serious happen to her? Should I call her? No, I want to meet her. Did it happen because of me? Because I walked out of her life?

My eyes welled up with tears. I tried to hold them back, pretending that everything was fine. I said a rushed goodbye to Maira and headed back home. While travelling, I couldn't understand what to do. I was panicking. I didn't care about what Ashna had done to me; I just wanted to see her

I immediately booked a flight from Mumbai to Delhi. I just wanted to get to Delhi as fast as I could.

16

The Realization

Samar

When I landed in Delhi after many months, I felt ecstatic. In fact, when I looked down from the window of my plane, just when it was about to land, I was delighted because I was coming back to the place where I belonged.

I had landed at 4 a.m. and was standing outside Terminal 3 at Indira Gandhi airport, waiting for dawn to break because I had nowhere to go. I had neither informed at home nor Kartik that I was visiting Delhi. All I wanted to do was see Ashna.

I wasn't complaining because it felt nice to be at the airport. I observed people who had come to drop off or pick up their loved ones. I witnessed both the pain of separation and the joy of reunion.

It struck me to capture all these emotions in a cartoon. I took out a pen and my pocket diary to put my thoughts on paper. Then, I looked around for inspiration. I decided to illustrate a group of friends who had come to see off one of their friends. They caught my attention because I could relate to them. Their captivating laughter made me reminisce my college days when Ashna, Kartik, Sakshi and I used to have so much of fun.

Just as I had begun to draw, I heard their laughter stop. I looked up to see that a girl, who had to leave, started embracing her friends. I understood that the time of separation had come. I had no clue why she was leaving, but I could sense her agony.

I couldn't stop thinking about the pain that I experienced due to the separation from my best friend. I had chosen to go away from her. How foolish of me!

Doesn't love mean to let go? Doesn't it mean that you let the person you love find their happiness? Maira's words started echoing in my mind.

Have I always been a self-centred person? Did I befriend Ashna only because I wanted to be in a relationship with her? Did I never care for her as the best friend I always claim to be? These questions erupted in my mind, followed by immense guilt.

Maira was right when she said love was about giving, but all I ever did was to pressurize Ashna into loving me. I couldn't fool myself anymore. I am a horrible person.

I started questioning my life choices, but I understood that it was the right time to forget the past and start things anew.

She needs me, and I must go back and apologize to her. The time that I lost cannot come back, but now I won't waste any more minutes and I will bring my best friend back in my life. I will correct everything forever.

Ashna

I regained consciousness in a hospital, amidst the smell of antiseptics.

I lay surrounded by people dressed in pale yellow clothes. When I had fallen off the bike, sliding across the rugged road, the left part of my body was bruised because of scraping against the concrete. Thus, I had cuts and scratches near my left cheekbone and severe swelling around that area.

My left hand and leg were typically black and blue because of the underlying blood clots. However, one major cause of concern was the fracture in my left leg, precisely on the last toe which had displaced outwards due to the impact. After a while, the doctor discharged me, advising me to take complete bed rest for two to three weeks.

Since then, I had been at home, confined to bed. My mother had cried when she saw me limping back home. She wouldn't sleep unless she was sure that I had fallen asleep peacefully. Along with her, my father also made sure to spend time with me. He would sit beside my bed almost every day, talking to me and easing my pain. Sometimes, he tried to probe into how the accident had occurred, but I could never bring myself to revealing the truth.

Being bedridden, I had a lot of free time, so most of the time, my mind would wander into the past. Through some deep introspection, I realized that life is kind and generous and it always gives us an opportunity which forces us to reflect on our choices. I knew I stood at that particular fork in life when I had to introspect.

One night, I suddenly realized that right before the accident, when Aman had kissed me and had given me the ring, I was terribly confused whether I loved him or not.

I was finally able to accept that each of the decisions that I had taken after my graduation dinner were a result of panic and confusion. I acted in haste, without really thinking about my choices and worrying about their consequences. Everything that I had done, right from the graduation night to accepting Aman's ring haunted me.

Apparently, Aman had not suffered from any major injuries. He was worried about me and he would make a visit every three to four days. Though he would message every day and ask me whether I wanted him to come over and spend some time with him, I never felt like talking to him anymore. In fact, I struggled to accept that I had been missing Samar a lot, especially after the accident.

Why am I feeling this way? Why do I want Samar to be here with me? Maybe because I want my best friend's support now or perhaps, I just wanted to talk to someone who's been so close. But then, why am I not talking to Aman or to my parents? They are the closest to me. Why does Aman not seem important? Is it because of the professional relationship that we have? Or is it something else? Damn! What are my feelings? What do I want?

Maybe my diary could help me figure out what I wanted!

I immediately asked my mother to bring it from my cupboard. As soon as she brought it, I opened it and flipped through the pages, nostalgia running through my head. Finally, my eyes stopped on a page where I had described my experiences and feelings on the day of our Graduation Dinner.

Every entry that I read from that diary caused an emotional outburst within me. In the three hours that followed, I cherished every little memory from the time I had spent with Samar and my friends, realizing how invaluable they were. Samar was my friend. I still don't know what I had with him, but I was sure of one thing – whatever I had with Aman was not love.

I realized that I had been an immature girl, who never took decisions on her own. It was always dictated by circumstances. Perhaps my actions were nothing but a means of escaping the truth.

But, that's enough! I am done with making excuses. Not everybody gets a chance to introspect and correct their mistakes. I'm glad I broke some bones; it helped me plaster my broken life. At least now I know which boat I have to sail on.

I closed my diary and laid back. I was ready to face what lay ahead of me.

❖

Tring!

It was ten in the morning when the doorbell rang. It was seldom that we had an early visitor. As I was lying down comfortably on my bed, I heard my name.

'Ashna!' My mother called for me, 'someone is here to see you.'

'Who is it ma?' I asked, even though I knew it would be Aman because he was the only person who visited me these days. This was something that didn't excite me. In fact, I deliberately curled up inside the quilt and closed my eyes, pretending to sleep. But then, I heard a familiar voice.

'Hi Ashna!'

I knew it wasn't Aman's because it gave me goose bumps. I couldn't believe my ears. I opened my eyes, removed the quilt and got up. And there he stood, right in front of me.

'Samar?' I spoke, my voice weak and feeble, as I could barely lift my eyes to look up at him.

It was hard to face each other. I felt a lump in my throat as I tried to speak, so I chose not to. My eyes filled up as I looked into his. I felt like jumping up from my bed to hug him. But, I couldn't break away from his gaze. I wanted that moment to freeze for some time because I felt happy, relieved and complete. There was an inexplicable bliss in his presence. I felt secure and loved, even though he hadn't said a word to me.

However, it was hard to begin a conversation. We had three-and-a-half months' worth of sharing to do, but still, we just couldn't talk. Although both of us were the same people, who were best friends once, awkwardness had seeped in between us.

Isn't it funny how two people, who were once closest to each other and could talk for hours, were not able to initiate a simple conversation? It was the strangest feeling. On the one hand, I was thrilled to have Samar back in my life. But, on the other hand, I felt uneasy because I couldn't muster courage to speak in front of him.

'How are you?' Samar asked, breaking the unusual silence between us. His voice was coarse. I could clearly see that he was very sentimental.

'Fine,' I said softly. 'What about you, how are you?' I managed to ask him.

'Good,' he replied and smiled for a very brief moment.

'How is Mumbai?' I continued, hoping to carry forward the conversation and reduce the awkwardness.

'You knew I was in Mumbai, Ashna?'

'Yes, I keep a tab on you. In fact, I still follow you everywhere you go,' I spoke, hoping to lighten the mood.

'Sure, as if you have time to do that,' he sneered and I understood the underlying taunt he had made. But, I was happy that my Samar was back.

'You can clearly see that I do have a lot of time,' I said gesturing towards my broken foot.

I tried to stand up taking the support of my crest, but Samar stooped in towards me and put my hand around his shoulder to support me.

'What do you need, tell me?' he asked.

'Nothing, I just wanted to hug you,' I said, realizing that I had not planned it.

He looked up at me and then, took me into a slight embrace, a side hug basically. It was a soothing and exciting touch. It felt disturbing when he moved away. Maybe, I wanted to be in my best friend's embrace for a little longer.

'Ashna, I know that I have been a complete idiot in the past few months. I shouldn't have walked out of your life. I am sorry,' he spoke, all of a sudden.

'No, it wasn't your fault,' I said but he interrupted me before I could complete what I was saying.

'It was my fault. I had no right to abandon you just because you felt differently. You had never said that you loved me. You had never given me any false hopes. In fact, you were always honest in our friendship. It was I who always craved for more. After all, what was your fault if you loved someone else? I should not have broken our friendship, no matter what. Best friends don't do that,' he looked apologetically at me.

'But, let's forget what's done. I want our friendship back. I want us to be the same old Samar and Ashna who were important to each other,' he ended, looking hopefully at me.

'You were always important to me. You never ceased to be my best friend, Samar. Nothing could ever make you less important in my life, nothing,' I said, wiping away a tiny drop of tear from the corner of my eye. These were tears of peace.

'Samar, you can't take the entire blame on yourself,' I began to explain to him when I heard another voice.

'Ashna?' Samar and I turned to look at that person. I already knew who it was. Aman!

'I hope I am not interrupting,' he said, smiling.

'No, please come,' I said hesitatingly, as I looked at Samar, while addressing Aman.

'Aman this is Samar, my friend and Samar, this is Aman,' I introduced them, avoiding using the word boyfriend anywhere.

They greeted each other warmly, but I knew Samar wasn't comfortable. Aman didn't know much about him, while Samar knew everything about Aman.

'So, Samar, are you Ashna's college friend?' Aman asked.

'Yes,' Samar replied with a smile, but I could feel that it wasn't genuine.

Again, I tried to get up from my bed, but this time Aman jumped to help me. I noticed that Samar too had moved with the intention to help me, but he stopped looking at Aman. In my heart, I felt strange, because I wanted Samar to hold me, and not Aman. Somehow, my boyfriend didn't seem as close to me as my best friend.

'I think I should leave now. I have to go and meet some of my friends,' Samar said casually, but I understood why he wanted to leave all of a sudden. We couldn't even complete talking about our friendship. Aman had interrupted before we could.

Why did Aman come? Couldn't he have come a little later? I want to be with Samar for some time, but now he is leaving. I should stop him.

'We have met after so long, can't you stay a little longer?' I asked, hoping that he wouldn't deny.

'No, I am here only for a day. I have to go home and then meet other people as well,' he said and turned away to leave.

I couldn't muster the courage to stop him. I felt as if Aman's presence, and that heavy ring that rested on my finger had restricted me from doing so.

This whole episode had cleared my mind. In fact, it had completed what my diary had started. I had figured out a reason to listen to my heart, something that I was trying to search in my diary.

I knew what my heart wanted and I could not feel happier.

17

The Shocking Revelation

Ashna

'That's it! Stop right there near that black gate,' I instructed the cab driver as he drove past a few bungalows and flats in B-block, Preet Vihar in East Delhi.

Almost eight days after Samar had visited me, I got my plaster removed. Although I had not recovered completely and my mom had been angry because I was sneaking out of the house, I couldn't stop. I had to make things right.

I was here to meet Aman.

I knew what I was about to do was wrong, but it had to be done. For the first time in my life, I was choosing courage over convenience. I was listening to the rhythm of my heart, rather than the logic of my mind.

I rang the bell of his house and patiently waited for someone to open the door.

'Who is it?' Aman's sister asked. Before I could answer, Aman opened the door.

'You?' he asked, looking startled.

His reaction was obvious because he wasn't expecting me. I had not told him that I was coming over to his place. He looked different from usual. His hair was messed up and he wore a plain gray t-shirt with a pair of joggers.

'What are you doing here?' he asked, pleasantly surprised at my arrival. A soft smile slowly crept on his face. I smiled back at him because I didn't have an answer to his question.

What was I doing here at his doorstep?

Even after reading my diary, I was confused about many things, especially related to Samar. However, I understood one thing very clearly – I didn't love Aman. I had known this from the beginning, but I had ignored it, thinking that love needed time to grow. But I was wrong. Samar's visit worked as the final nail in the coffin because I realized that my relationship with Aman suffocated me. He was a nice guy and I was not what he deserved. Therefore, I decided to break up with him.

'I wanted to see you so I thought if I could visit,' I lied, right on his face.

'Ashna,' he replied lovingly, 'you could have told me, I would have come. Anyway, please come in,' he said, moving aside and allowing me to step into his house.

'Please sit,' he said as he gestured towards the couch.

I looked around while settling down. His house looked immaculate.

'Tanvi, can you bring some water please?' he called out his sister. Soon she walked in with a glass of water. She greeted me with a smile and then went away.

'What would you like to have, coffee or tea?' he asked, blushing each time he looked at me.

I don't want anything. I just want to break up with you, I am sorry.

'Coffee would do,' I replied slowly, avoiding his friendly gaze.

'Thank god you said coffee because I don't know how to make tea. Tanvi has semester exams and I didn't want to disturb her,' he said giggling.

Since the kitchen was attached to the living room, he could chat with me while he prepared coffee. He asked me about my health. I replied to all his questions very mechanically as my mind wasn't really involved in the interaction. I was trying to steer the conversation in a way that I could talk about the break up.

Suddenly, a vintage marble telephone that was kept on the cabinet caught my eye. It had a round dial which made a clicking sound every time one dialled a number by pressing and rotating it. It was kept as a showpiece but the child in me wanted to touch it. So, I stood up and started exploring it. There were other things on the cabinet – a small blue crystal turtle, a white porcelain idol of laughing Buddha, and one of those customized mugs on which pictures are printed. As I lifted the mug to see the picture, I felt strange. It was almost as if I had seen that picture before.

The picture had two happy kids – a little boy was wearing his school uniform and the cute girl was wearing a fancy yellow dress. The two kids were holding each other's hands. It was an adorable picture and I had a hunch that I had seen this picture before. But where? I dived further in my memories and searched every corner of my mind, but I still couldn't remember anything.

'Ashna, coffee is ready,' Aman called out as he put down a tray filled with two coffee mugs and a bowl of masala potato wafers on the centre table.

I took a sip and smiled at him, gesturing that the coffee was good. The time had come when I had to break the news to him. As soon as I was about to begin, my eyes wandered around the room and I started looking at the mug again. Suddenly, I remembered where I had seen that picture.

I put the coffee mug back on the tray and rushed to grab the picture mug. Aman was confused at my behaviour.

This is not Tanvi, but how is this possible?

What is happening here? What is her picture doing here?

I was shocked because I couldn't understand what Maira's picture was doing in Aman's house.

I recalled the day when we were supposed to meet with the clients from Vericon Builders at the Royal Plaza. When Maira had not showed up, and I had texted her on WhatsApp to know about her whereabouts, this picture had been her display picture back then.

It was the same girl who was there on the picture mug at Aman's house. 'Is this you?' I asked Aman, pointing towards the boy in the picture.

'Yes, and that is Maira next to me,' he replied making a sorry face.

I stared at him in disbelief.

Maira and Aman know each other since childhood? How was this possible? How come they never told me or anyone at the office? Did they hide it intentionally? What was their relationship?

I was clearly very disturbed by this discovery and it felt as if every vein in my head was about to explode.

'What? How long have you known each other? Seems like since childhood,' I said, in a sarcastic tone. I don't know why, but I felt betrayed.

'Yes, and I've been meaning to tell you this from a long time. In fact, do you remember that I wanted to tell you something, right before that accident happened? This is what it was. Maira and I are childhood friends. In fact, we are best friends,' he completed.

Maira and Aman were childhood best friends? Was he kidding me?

'How come nobody knows about it in the office?' I asked, looking directly at him.

'That's because we didn't want people to know about us. Maira wasn't very comfortable with it. She felt that it would make people judge her as everyone would believe that she got the job because of me,' he said

Wait, maybe he is right! I started arranging every piece of this puzzle in my mind.

Soon, I understood how everything had always been right in front of my eyes, but I had never noticed any of it. Everything made sense. I understood why Maira never shared much about her life or why she came to Aman's rescue when someone made fun of him. Not because they were in love as I had once presumed, but because they were best friends.

'Okay, I can understand why you didn't tell people at the office, but why didn't you tell me? I was your girlfriend; then why didn't any of you tell me? Was I not worthy of being trusted? Did she ask you not to do so? Does she not like me? Yeah, that's why she never shared anything with me,' I went on babbling, not realizing how I was feeling really angry.

'Ashna, that's not the case,' said Aman. 'you are getting it all wrong, because Maira likes you a lot. In fact, Maira was the reason why we are together. She brought us closer,' he said, sounding worried at how I was reacting to the news. *Maira has brought us closer? Is he talking about the suggestion she gave me to get committed with him? Did she tell him about it?*

'What? You know about what she has done?' I asked him naively.

'Of course, she's been my love guru throughout,' he replied innocently.

What was he talking about?

Perhaps, he read my expression because he continued, 'Ashna, everything that has happened between us – starting from the meeting at the Royal Plaza to the ring I gave you the other day... everything was planned by Maira. She was the mastermind behind our love story,' he said, smiling at me.

'Aman, please, can you be specific? I am not able to understand you,' I said as I looked at him confused.

'See, I started having feelings for you ever since you were training under me. But, I didn't have the guts to tell you, so I told Maira about it. She assured me that she would find a way for me to reach you. And she did! That meeting at the Royal Plaza wasn't an official meeting. Biztech had already closed a deal with Vericon a week before that. It was basically a date that Maira had arranged for us so that I could tell you about my feelings. That's why she didn't show up and she didn't even let Rajat come because she called and told him that the meeting had been cancelled,' he said, explaining in detail.

Was that meeting fake? Maira set everything up? Why was he so happy about it?

'Not only that meeting, but even that ring was Maira's idea,' he said, gesturing towards my hand. 'She was the one who got it made on special order. And then, got it parcelled to Delhi. I just had to pick it up and gift it to you,' he continued.

He came close to me and cupped my face in his hands, 'See, she loves you, otherwise why do you think she would have done this much for us?' he asked, looking directly into my eyes.

I was stupefied. Aman obviously thought that Maira's role was limited to his side of the story, but he didn't know that she was a key player in my story as well. In fact, Maira was really a mastermind in a game where Aman, Samar and I were just pawns. She had known everything all along.

When I went to her to get advice on Samar's possessiveness, whatever she said provoked me to get into a relationship with

Aman. All this time, I thought that she was being a friend to me, but in reality, she was being a friend only to Aman.

Why did she do this to me? Why would she try to sabotage my friendship with Samar? Did she do it for Aman? I had absolutely no idea where my life was going.

What about the break-up? I realized that I had forgotten about it.

Think of a valid reason, the fact that you don't love him isn't convincing enough. What if I break up with him because he has been hiding the truth about Maira from a long time? The explanation seemed plausible.

'Aman,' I said slowly, pulling his ring out of my finger, 'I don't think I want to be in this relationship anymore,' I said at last, after hesitating for a couple of minutes.

He just stared at me. He was perplexed; perhaps he couldn't believe that I was breaking up with him. I felt bad for him.

'What are you saying, Ashna? Do you... want to break up?' he uttered.

'Yes, we have trust issues and I think you know why. You kept hiding things from me for so long. Relationships don't work this way. Trust is the foundation of a fulfilling relationship. You didn't trust me and now, I won't be able to trust you. So, it'll be better if we break up,' I said, handing him the ring.

It wasn't as easy as I had presumed it to be. We argued for at least two hours. He apologized, trying to give reasons to make me stay. But after a point, he understood my perspective.

I didn't know whether I had done the right things or not. All I knew was that I felt like a free bird who had escaped the cage that she had been trapped in. It was liberating.

18

The Confrontation

Ashna

Why did Maira do this to me?

I didn't have the patience to go home and call her. Had it been in my hands, I would have made her stand in front of me and fired questions like bullets from a gun. She was lucky to have been far away, as she was safe from my wrath. I went to a nearby park and called her up.

'Look who has called me! I think you have dialled a wrong number Ashna,' jibed Maira answering her call. 'How are you?' she continued, after composing herself a little.

Trapped! I am trapped in your cobweb of lies and intricate plans.

'I am fine, and you?' I asked her, trying to keep the conversation normal.

'I am good. In fact, I am too good. First, you tell me why didn't you call me from such a long time? Okay, forget it! I'm just glad that you called. You know I was about to call you myself because I wanted to tell you something,' she said.

I was surprised. She has never shared anything before, then why did she want to do it today? Maybe she wants to make a confession.

'Really, what is it?' I continued normally.

'Okay,' she took a sigh and began, 'you know a few days ago, I bumped into someone,' she continued.

She met someone, and how is this related to whatever she did to me? Is she telling me something else, isn't she making a confession?

'Who?' I blurted.

'Samar!' she said jovially. I was surprised at the turn of events.

She met Samar, but where? Is she further trying to jeopardize my relationship with him?

'You met Samar? Aren't you in Pune and he in Mumbai? How did you people meet?' I was shocked.

'What can I say? This world is such a small place, Ashna. I was in Pune, but a few weeks ago, my classes got shifted to Mumbai and guess what! I met Samar and that too, on Tinder. Can you believe it? Two people who were from Delhi bump into each other in Mumbai! Luck, right?' she said while I could feel the joy she was experiencing.

I didn't like it. She continued, 'We talked and then, we decided to meet. I can't tell you how awesome our first meeting was. We really connected. Then we started meeting regularly. I can't explain how I feel when I'm with him. I just love his company and I am sure he loves mine too. I can see…' she paused for a second and then continued, 'why he is your best friend. He is perfect,' she completed with a sigh.

I felt a twitch in my gut. My face became warm and drops of sweat broke out on my forehead. I didn't like the fact that she met Samar. Was I getting insecure of Maira and possessive for Samar?

'You mean, you people have become friends?' I asked hesitantly.

'Not just friends, Ashna. Mumbai has made us the best of friends. I hope you are okay with it?' she asked so tenderly that I couldn't believe that she was the same person who had messed up my life.

I didn't have any reason to not agree with her. I couldn't ask her to stop hanging out with Samar just because she had wronged me. I didn't have a right to take decisions for Samar, even though I didn't feel good about Maira being around Samar. I didn't want to be perceived as an overly insecure person.

'Yes, why wouldn't I be?' I lied.

'I thought that since Samar and I both are your friends, you might feel awkward that I am befriending him behind your back. But, thank god you don't have any issue. I am happy. Wait, let me send you our pictures,' she said and before I could say anything, I had already received WhatsApp messages from her.

All the pictures that she sent were of them taking selfies, with food on their plates. In some of them, Maira even had her hand around Samar's shoulder. I could see that they were happy, but I wasn't.

Am I really jealous of her?

'Nice,' I replied plainly.

I decided to drop confronting Maira. Those pictures were proof that Samar was happy with her and I realized that no matter how angry I was with her, it was time to let it go. I tried to forget whatever she had done to me, consoling myself that maybe she wasn't that wrong. It was because she had done everything for her best friend. I couldn't blame her for everything, because even though she had influenced me, all the decisions that I had taken were a result of my own judgement.

'How is Samar, by the way?' I asked her, quite involuntarily.

I didn't know how Samar really was. When he had visited me the last time and we had decided to revive our friendship, he had left abruptly. I couldn't gather enough courage to call him up and apologize for letting him go away. We hadn't spoken after that.

'He is good, except for the fact that he has been trying hard to get a job in cartooning, but hasn't received any offer yet,' she said.

I felt extremely happy for Samar after hearing that he was finally trying to get into a job that he always wanted. I was glad that Samar was taking this risk and I was confident that he just needed a chance to prove himself in order to be successful. Taking a plunge into what someone is passionate about is the most courageous thing to do.

'But, why are his cartoons being rejected? Did he tell you the reason? I mean, does he know where he's going wrong?' I replied. I wanted to know what was holding back Samar's creative instincts.

'No, even he doesn't have a clue. He told me that he always tried to mould himself according to the taste of the publishers. He studies the kinds of cartoons they publish and draws his cartoons accordingly,' she replied.

'Wait, what if they don't want the cartoons of the same kind? What if they are looking for something original?' I said, but I immediately regretted saying it aloud.

You should have told this directly to Samar. Now she will tell this to him and you will lose a point.

'Yes! This might be the reason. He believes that the publishers are looking for a particular style, but maybe all they need is an original idea,' she continued.

I could sense excitement in her voice.

'Yes, and I have something that can help him,' I said forgetting once again that I was not supposed to spill out my ideas to Maira.

'What?' she asked excitedly.

'I have one of his original cartoons. I will send that to him and I am sure wherever he will submit that, people will love it,' I replied confidently.

I remembered the doodle that he had created that day when we met at café Cheeros. Samar did not show that illustration to me because he had been angry with me. Since I wanted to see it, I had grabbed it and put it into my bag.

I never let him know that I had preserved it with me all this time.

'May I see it?' she asked, perhaps curious to hop onto this opportunity to impress him.

'I don't think I have it with me right now. I'll send it to you when I reach home,' I lied, even though I had a picture of that cartoon on my phone. I had no intention of sending it to her because I wanted to send it to Samar and make him feel special.

'Okay Maira, bye. I'll talk to you later,' I said and decided to hang up, because I wanted to go home and send that cartoon to Samar at the earliest. I believed that it would give our friendship a second chance.

'Ashna wait! Listen,' she said just when I was about to cut the call.

'Yes?' I continued.

'There is one more thing that I want you to know,' she said hesitantly.

'Ashna, I like Samar and I want to get into a relationship with him,' she blurted out rapidly, taking a sigh of relief thereafter.

It took me some seconds to register what she had said. I could not believe that Maira had something like this in mind.

How could she like Samar? She barely knew him for some weeks.

'You just met him a few weeks ago,' I said reluctantly.

'I know, but is the duration of the relationship really important? I mean, we love each other's company and I like spending time with him. Isn't that enough? You can fall in love in a second. You got into a relationship with Aman after knowing him for just two months. How does one decide the right time to fall in love, Ashna?'

'Does Samar know about how you feel for him?' I asked, hoping to hear that he had already rejected her.

'No, I was planning on telling him tomorrow. Though, I am sure that he will accept my proposal,' she said.

No! This can't be happening.

Tears started rolling down my cheeks inadvertently. I hung up on her and instantly switched off my phone. I didn't want to cry, but my tears were unstoppable.

Why are you crying? It's not as if you love Samar or have feelings for him. You never loved him. You wanted him to move on. And now when he is moving on, then why are you crying? Are you being insecure? I don't understand. Maybe, it is because this is going to mark an end to Samar and Ashna. But didn't everything end the day you chose Aman over him?

After a while, I composed myself and switched on my phone. As soon as I did that, I received a call from Maira again. I knew that my voice had become husky, but I tried to keep my cool while speaking to her.

'What happened?' she asked, sounding worried.

'Nothing, my phone fell from my hand and the battery got detached,' I lied.

'It's fine. So, what's your opinion on whatever I said? Wait, let me guess, obviously you must be happy about it because finally Samar will be moving on and he will be getting someone who loves him. This is what you always wanted, right?' she asked, leaving me confused, because even though she was right, it still didn't feel right.

'Yes,' I replied slowly.

'Thank you so much Ashna, because this means a lot. Now I need a favour from you. Can you please send that illustration to me and allow me to give it to Samar? I know you wanted to give it to him, but I want to confess my feelings with it. I hope you won't mind,' she spoke softly, almost pleading me.

I was compelled to accept her request. After all, she was about to get into a more intimate relationship with Samar than what I had with him. Quite unwillingly, I sent her that illustration. Just as I clicked the 'send' button, I felt a sense of loss within me.

Something was slipping out of my hand, leaving behind total darkness. Maybe Samar was my only ray of light.

19

The Celebration

Samar

Why did she call me here?

I was strolling near Marine Drive, waiting for Maira and admiring the spell-binding skyline of Mumbai which was glittering against the night sky. Since we always met at some café or restaurant, I was surprised when she asked me to meet her at Marine Drive. I didn't know much about her except for the fact that she used to work at Biztech with Ashna and was pursuing a course in film-making, I was still fond of our meetings.

I chose a spot to sit, along the edge of the promenade of Marine Drive, facing the sea and listening to the calm rustle of the approaching and retreating waves. I closed my eyes as I tried to concentrate on that soothing sound that took my mind away from the noise of the traffic nearby.

Before I could have lost myself in that rhythm, Maira's voice cut through my thoughts. I turned around to see her standing there, looking gorgeous in an elegant black jumpsuit. On the contrary, I was dressed in a casual red shirt and blue denims.

'Hey,' I said, getting up to hug her. 'Are you coming straight out of a party?' I asked noticing her long silver earrings with black stones.

'No,' she replied, looking at me with a weird look on her face.

'No? Then, did you dress up just to meet me?' I asked curiously.

'Yes,' she blushed. 'Is that a problem?' she smiled back at me.

'Yes, you look absolutely stunning,' I replied.

'Thanks,' she responded, blushing to herself.

'Shall we go to some café?' I asked her, gesturing to leave.

'Yes, we will, but can't we sit here for some time?' she asked, sitting down on the promenade.

'Yeah, why not? This is one of my favourite places in Mumbai,' I replied and sat down next to her. It felt weird.

Did Maira really call me to Marine Drive just to sit here?

'Tell me one thing, what's your take on relationships?' she asked.

I was puzzled. I didn't know what exactly she meant when she asked 'your take on relationships'. Still, I struggled to say something, but she interrupted before I could say anything.

'Wait, before you say anything, I have something that belongs to you,' she said, taking out her phone. She surfed through her phone's gallery and stopped and forwarded her phone towards me. I looked at the picture, which left me bewildered.

'This... is my illustration,' I spoke out loud, amazed because it was the same that I had drawn while waiting for Ashna at Cafe Cheeros in Delhi. As far as I remembered, I had crumbled it and thrown it away.

'Where did you find it?' I asked her excitedly.

'I got it from somewhere and I liked it, so I had kept it carefully with me. I have the original one back at home. I will give it you when we will be in Delhi. Till then, you can have this picture,' she said in a peppy voice.

'Oh! Now I get it! You have this illustration with you because you were there at Cafe Cheeros that day. Perhaps you had picked it up from where it was lying crumbled and kept it with you, right?' I said, feeling proud of having solved that mystery.

'Exactly, that's what happened,' she replied.

I couldn't control myself and hugged her, thanking her profusely for preserving it.

'No! Don't thank me, Samar. I had forgotten that I had it with me. But when you told me that you were being rejected again and again, suddenly this beautiful illustration came to my mind. You know what? I think you should send this to every magazine and newspaper. They might accept an original illustration like this,' she said earnestly.

She insisted on sending that cartoon to the publishers right away. Due to her encouragement, I sent it to every single newspaper and magazine that I was trying to reach out to.

How ironic is this! Being my best friend, I had wanted Ashna to see my cartoon, but she didn't really care. And Maira, whom I had barely known at that time, had preserved it with her.

'I can't thank you enough Maira, you don't know how much you have helped me by reminding me of this,' I said.

'Samar, please! There is no need to mention it again. By the way, now you can tell me what is your take on relationships?' she said, making me quite uneasy.

'I can't say how much I know about relationships, because I only liked Ashna throughout my college life. But you already know that I could never get into a relationship with her. Then, I didn't get another chance,' I replied, quite frankly.

'So, all you need is another chance, right?' she continued. Her eyes were gleaming with excitement.

'I don't know whether I am ready to take that leap or not?' I said, looking down at the sea.

'No, you just said that you never got a chance. So, I think you just need a chance,' she probed.

'Maybe, Maira! But, why do you want to know about my opinion on relationships?'

'Umm... because I want to be that chance for you Samar,' she paused. 'I love you!'

'What! You love me?' I asked her with a sense of shock.

'Yes,' she replied, looking down. 'I love you.'

'Maira, we hardly know each other,' I said tenderly, not wanting to hurt her.

'So what Samar?' she said, standing up and raising her voice.

'Since when did love have to depend on parameters like time? I just know that I love you and even if it is wrong, I don't care. I don't know whether this city made me fall in love with you or the fact that I found peace in your company. All I know is that I look forward to meeting you. Isn't that enough to fall in love?' she entreated.

I kept staring at her in disbelief. Even though I had made myself believe that I had moved on and was ready for a change, in reality, I wasn't. Even if I didn't love Ashna anymore, that didn't mean that I was ready to take this leap.

'Maira, you love me, and that is very generous of you,' I said, loathing myself at the choice of words. 'I mean, it's great that you feel this way about me and you are terrific. But I don't think I am ready to get into a relationship yet,' I spoke slowly.

'Why?' she said, clearly disappointed.

'You know too well that I am trying to get over Ashna. I don't think it would be a good idea to get into a relationship before I completely move on from her,' I said frankly.

'And, when is that going to happen?' she retorted.

'I am not sure about it,' I replied.

'You'll never be sure about it, Samar. Because somewhere deep down, you love this emptiness and the inexplicable pain,' she said.

'What are you saying? That's not true,' I defended.

'Yes, it is. And if it's not, then why are you not giving this relationship a chance? Why won't you give me a chance? Samar, you are doing exactly what Ashna did to you. You are friend-zoning me,' she said.

This compelled me to think.

Was I really friend-zoning her? She had been a good friend. But I don't like her that way, and she is just a friend. Oh no! I am really friend-zoning her! How can I do that to someone when I know how it feels to be friend-zoned.

I was petrified because I didn't know what to do.

'No, I don't want to friend-zone you,' I said, feeling embarrassed.

'You won't. Just give this relationship a chance, Samar,' she said and took my hand into hers.

Her touch felt strangely comforting. On one hand, my heart didn't approve of Maira, but on the other, my mind felt that it was right. After all, I had always longed to be loved passionately. I was confused. So, for the time being, I thought it was best to acknowledge her feelings.

'Fine,' I said reluctantly, smiling back at her.

'Fine? Does that mean that you are accepting this relationship?' she jumped up with joy.

'Yes,' I replied slowly, because I wasn't as excited as she was.

'Thank you Samar! I know our love story won't remain incomplete,' she whispered in my ears while being in my embrace.

'Good! Now, can we can go to some place and eat?' I asked.

'No, we won't go and *just eat*. We are newly committed in this relationship. This calls for a celebration. Let's go to a place where we can party and get wasted,' she said, winking at me and giving me a naughty smile.

I wasn't very keen on that idea as I was not very fond of drinking. But I was not able to change her mind.

'I know a perfect place to celebrate this day,' she said, waving towards a local taxi. 'Lower Parel,' she said to the driver. He nodded and we sat in the car.

Did she already know that we were going to party? Is that why she was dressed like this?

'Where are we going?' I asked.

'Todi Mill Social,' she replied.

Throughout the journey, she held my hand and passed me intermittent smiles. We got down from the taxi and walked up to the lounge. I don't know why, but I was getting somewhat anxious.

When I got into Todi Mill Social, I was in awe of the ambience of that place. We had to wait for some time to get a table. As soon as we got one, Maira called the waiter and whispered into his ears. She asked me if it would be okay to have Italian. I nodded. I wasn't interested in knowing what she had ordered. After a while, a waiter laid a bowl of nachos, Mac and Cheese and a large cylindrical glass with a colourful drink that didn't seem like beer at all.

'What is this?' I asked, pointing towards the glass.

'Classic LIIT pitcher, the perfect alcohol to give this evening a nice kick,' she replied coolly.

'Cheers to our new beginning!' she exclaimed exuberantly.

I smiled and we took a few sips from the pitcher. I liked its tangy and bitter-sweet flavour. Soon, its taste grew upon me and I was craving for more after every sip. I noticed that Maira was taking it slow.

Halfway through the pitcher, the alcohol started affecting me. My senses had become dull and a certain lightness gushed all over me. I liked this feeling.

Why hadn't I ever felt like this before? Maybe because I had never drank this much alcohol before. This feels great. Maybe destiny wanted me to get into a relationship with Ashna, oops Maira. Who knows, maybe Ashna was never my destiny, and Maira is.

I looked at Maira, but she seemed sober.

'I think destiny wanted me to be here at this moment,' I said and raised my glass.

'Cheers to us! Now, I will count to three and we will have bottoms up, okay?' she said, and showed me thumbs up.

'Three!' she began. I didn't even wait for her to start and started drinking incessantly. Eventually, I emptied the entire pitcher.

By the end of the session, I could barely stand. It was difficult to hold my head up straight. The world around me looked hazy. I was so hammered that at one point of time, I even forgot that I was at Social and had gone there with Maira.

Thereafter, I remembered the next set of events in snapshots. I remember being in a cab, but I had no clue where I was going. I remember a girl sitting beside me and holding my arm. We reached somewhere but I had no clue where I was. Maira helped me to get out of the cab. Then, I found myself struggling to climb the stairs by taking her support.

Next moment, I was in a room lying shirtless on a sofa. Maira got on top of me and planted a kiss on my lips. Although, my subconscious was aware that I didn't want to do it, but I couldn't oppose her. She kept kissing me and then, slowly unbuttoned my denims.

20

Destiny's Play

Samar

When I woke up the next morning, I had a very strong hangover. I could almost feel the bile rising up to my throat. I rubbed my eyes on my way to the washroom to throw up. It soon struck me that I wasn't at my aunt's place.

Where the hell am I?

I was in a room with a sofa on which I had woken up. A comforter was kept at one corner, tightly tucked at its foot. There was also a dressing table with some cabinets, along with a side table on which a lamp and a telephone was kept. The telephone directory indicated that we had to dial 119 to reach out to the reception desk. Upon reading it, I realized where I was.

This is a hotel! What was I doing in a hotel?

I tried to recall the events of the previous night, but I couldn't remember anything that happened after we were in the cab.

Why did I drink so much? I hated myself for overdoing it.

I splashed some water on my face and looked into the mirror. I noticed that I didn't have my shirt on and my denim was unbuttoned. Suddenly, flashes of Maira kissing me engulfed my mind.

We had sex! No, this can't happen.

I was petrified and denied my thoughts right away. But, I couldn't alter the truth. I might have been the only guy who loathed himself for getting laid with an extremely sexy girl. But this was different.

I didn't even want to be in a relationship in the first place. However, not only did I acknowledge my commitment to her but also got intimate with her. Could things be more messed up!

I came out of the bathroom, wondering where Maira was. She was not in the room when I had woken up. Perhaps she had left to attend her classes.

But, why didn't she wake me up? And why did she bring me here in the first place?

Maybe she left me a message. I had to scroll through my phone a bit to spot the message from Maira.

I forgot to inform my aunt. She must be panicking that I didn't reach home last night. I have to call her first and inform her that I am all right.

I found my phone lying on the dressing table. I checked out my notifications. There was just one missed call from my aunt. I rummaged through my call logs to look for any calls that I may have answered in my drunken state. Instead of that, I found a message that had been sent from my phone to my aunt.

"Sorry maasi, I am in a meeting right now and that's why I couldn't answer your call. Our company's owner has come for a special session. I will get late, so instead of coming home, I will stay at my friend's place. Don't worry! :-)"

When did I write that message?

I kept trying to recall the events of the night, but I just couldn't. I tried to call Maira many times, but I couldn't reach her.

I had a persistent headache which could only be combated with an espresso. I dressed up and walked out to pay for the night at the reception. When the receptionist told me that the room had been booked in advance and had already been paid for by Maira, I was surprised.

Why would Maira book a room in advance?

How did a single night become so mysterious for me?

'I am sorry I forgot something,' said the receptionist, opening a drawer and handing me a folded piece of paper from it.

'The girl who came with you last night left this for you,' she said.

'What is this?'

'I don't know, sir. She asked me to give it to you at check-out time,' she replied casually, shrugging.

'Okay, thank you so much,' I said as I took the paper from her.

Now, what is this? Was Maira some secret undercover agent? Does she want me to do something shady?

I brushed aside my thoughts and opened that piece of paper.

Samar,

I don't know how to put this, but I don't love you. I never did. I am extremely sorry. Everything I did till now was for my best friend. I don't know how much of it you will understand, but I will still try.

All I can tell you is that Ashna loves you. As a matter of truth, she has always loved you. That illustration which I gave you last night was not preserved by me. It was Ashna who had kept it all this time. She did it because she loved you. She might not even know this yet, but I am sure that she will eventually figure it all out.

Samar, you too have only loved her and nobody else stands a chance to replace her in your life. You two are meant for each other.

After reading this letter, please check the drafts in your message box and you will understand why I am saying this. I know I have wronged both you and Ashna. You guys trusted me, but all I ever did was to deceive you. But, I didn't have any choice. Just like you guys cared for each other, even I cared for my best friend, and all that I ever did was only for him.

However, now I realize that I shouldn't have played with your emotions. I shouldn't have tried to break your friendship with Ashna. I hope you will forgive me because you both know that for friends, we sometimes tend to take extreme measures.

Also, you won't be able to contact me, because I have blocked you from everywhere, so don't even try.

Hope your love finds its way.

Maira

P.S. We just kissed last night, and nothing else happened between us, so don't think too much about it.

❖

What is this? Am I part of some prank show? Are there any cameras around?

I had a severe headache and was utterly confused. That day was literally the most bizarre day of my life. I was dumped by my new girlfriend, in less than twelve hours.

Why did Maira get into a relationship with me if she wanted to dump me the next day? I was satisfied that I had some answers. I was relieved that we didn't have sex. But, the only problem was that Maira's explanation gave rise to trickier questions.

Who was the best friend that she was talking about? How was his life connected to Ashna and me? Why did she pretend to love me even when she didn't? What did she mean when she said that she had deceived Ashna as well? How did she break our friendship? Even if she did everything for a purpose, what made her confess it to me?

I read the letter once again to see if I could decipher anything from it, but all my efforts were futile. However, one thing caught my attention. Maira had written that Ashna had loved me, but how did she know this?

I already knew Ashna loved Aman, because he was her boyfriend, then why did Maira feel that Ashna loved me? Did Ashna tell her that she loved me? But, how could she suddenly start loving me if she couldn't for all these years?

Maira was close to her, and if she is saying this, then perhaps it means something. However, I am not sure how I can believe Maira on this, especially after she confessed how she had played us all along?

I think because now she doesn't have any reason to bluff us. Do I want to believe her?I don't love Ashna anymore, or do I? Is it because of my love for Ashna that I couldn't get into a relationship with Maira wholeheartedly?

I felt uneasy and depressed. Suddenly, I was reminded that in her letter, Maira had asked me to check the drafts folder of my message box, to understand why she said that I still loved Ashna.

There were six drafts and all were addressed to Ashna. I read them one after the other.

> ***Draft 1:*** *Ashna, I want to tell you that I love you. No one can love you like I do, not even your guy, Aman. No matter how much you deny it, but we are destined to be together. I may be your friend, but to me you are more than just a friend.*

Draft 2: *I feel alone without you. You know what, I am so drunk but I am still in my senses. I've felt so lonely without you all these months. I love you. Why can't you love me, Ashna?*

Draft 3: *I want to come back to you. I want to live every moment of our friendship again. I want us to go back to that happy place. I want to overcome all the complexities that have occurred between us. Why did this happen?*

Draft 4: *Please reply to me, Ashna. By the way, you know what, I keep telling everyone that I don't love you and that I don't need you. That's not true. You are everything I want from life.*

Draft 5: *Ashna, why are you not replying to my messages? Oh, why would you? I know you must be busy with Aman. He looks funny, though. He is the boyfriend and I am just the best friend. Boyfriends are more important. Why is your boyfriend more important when your best friend does everything for you?*

Draft 6: *You haven't replied to a single message Ashna. Can you tell me one thing why this happens… why do two best friends, who were once happy, cannot remain that way?*

Like everything else, I obviously couldn't recall when I had written those messages. I checked the sent folder but thankfully, I had not sent any of those messages to her.

Those messages were proof of what I wanted. I still loved Ashna and that was the truth. Maira had been right all along. All this was also very disturbing because I was back to the starting point. I loved her, but she didn't love me back.

I was sipping espresso while sitting in a CCD on my way to the office from that hotel. I had regained composure and I thought it was best to get back at work. From where I was, I could see my life getting even more complicated than before. Until last night, I just had to deal with my feelings for Ashna, but now I had to think about Maira and her best friend as well. Who was to be blamed for all this?

Of course, destiny! It was destiny that created further chaos in my life, rather than simplifying it. What do you want me to do!

Suddenly, I heard a beep on my phone which seemed to be the answer to my question. I hurriedly checked my phone, but it turned out be a work text from a colleague. Irritated, I was about to put my phone away when my eyes stopped on an email that I had ignored in the morning. I was just about to delete it as another spam email when something caught my attention.

Hello Samar,

We hope this message finds you in good health. This is regarding a cartoon submission you made to us earlier. We are glad to inform you that we found your piece original and informative and we would like to collaborate with you.

Creative minds are always welcome at Little Spot Publications. Please reply to this message at the earliest so that we can discuss further.

Sincerely,

Jyotsana Mukherjee
HR
Little Spot Publications

I was elated. I couldn't believe that Little Spot Publications had accepted my cartoon. They were one of the publishers I was trying to reach ever since I had started looking for a job as a cartoonist. However, they had never responded before, until that day. They had loved my illustration, "The Door" that Ashna had given to Maira, which I had sent a while back.

I felt so thankful to Ashna. I almost felt like hugging and kissing her right away. I didn't understand how these emotions had resurfaced inside me. I couldn't deny that Maira was equally responsible for this. She might have deceived me at some point, but if she hadn't pursued me to email it to the publishers then and there, I might have missed this opportunity.

Nevertheless, I immediately replied to Jyotsana, mentioning that I would love to work with them. She asked me if I was willing to participate in a small telephonic interview, and I promptly agreed. We spoke for about fifteen minutes, after which she was satisfied that cartooning was my passion and that I was right for the job. However, she did include that since I was a fresher, the company would first hire me on a probation period of two months. I agreed to it and was informed that I could join from the upcoming week in their Delhi office.

Destiny had finally heard my call. I was overwhelmed with happiness and excitement. Deep down, I knew that my life was about to change.

21

The Confession

Ashna

I was on my way back home from the office. Mom had called me in advance to inform me that she was preparing my favourite *matar paneer.* Ideally, I would have jumped with happiness because my mother's dishes were my favourite. But that day, it didn't matter. The feeling of happiness had vanished from my life.

Everything seemed uninteresting to me. An inexplicable anxiety shrouded my existence, making me feel dull and gloomy all the time. I didn't really have any definite explanation for it, but I knew for sure that it began the day Maira told me about Samar.

Since then, my mind was out of my control, picturing strange things related to both of them. I started imagining that they were holding hands and getting cosy in a car or in a room. I felt sick but I couldn't stop those images. At times, I even imagined them kissing each other passionately. I could not help but feel a sense of despair and loss.

Why should I care? Most probably, they were in a relationship. They were free to do whatever they wanted. If Samar was just a friend, then why was I not able to make peace with his relationship with Maira?

These thoughts were troubling my mind. I felt trapped and was looking for a way out. I wished that I hadn't lost all my friends at once because at that point, I needed them the most. Even my mom's matar paneer couldn't save me from this emotional turmoil. I just longed for a friend, who could help me and most importantly, listen to what I had to say.

I could smell the tempting aroma of mom's food from a distance. I rang the doorbell and waited for someone to open the door, but it wasn't my mom who opened it. Instead of her, some stranger opened the door. She had a classic bob haircut, brown vintage glasses and she was dressed in a pink sleeveless floral top with blue skinny jeans. She kept staring at me with a broad grin.

Who is she? Why is she passing me that broad smile?

Suddenly, I realized that the girl wasn't any stranger. She was someone who was very close to my heart and definitely an unexpected visitor.

'Sakshi? Oh my god! What have you done to your look?' I jumped to hug her. She looked so different, nothing like the Sakshi I had always known. Before going to Bengaluru, she was thinner and had long hair and she never wore glasses. However, now, she looked flamboyant and smart.

'So, finally you recognize me after taking an entire minute,' she said, feigning disappointment.

'Did you look at yourself in a mirror? You don't look like the Sakshi I knew. You look so hot. A more sophisticated version of yourself. What have you evolved into?' I said with a chuckle. 'More than that, what are you doing here in Delhi?'

'First of all, thanks for the compliments. I know I look hot,' she said, adjusting her glasses and making a pout.

'And secondly, I have come here on a break for three months. As soon as I landed here, I came to meet you because I was really missing you. I even called up at your landline and aunty told me that you were at the office. She told me she had made matar paneer so I came here running,' she completed, drawing a huge breath after speaking so much.

'Why didn't you call me then? I would have come home early,' I expressed.

'I was about to, but then, I thought of giving you a surprise!' she said, holding my hand and leading me into my own house.

'Bitch!' I said with affection and hugged her once again. Even though we had not talked or met each other in months, I was overjoyed to see her in front of me. She had entered back into my life, just at the right moment. It seemed as if all my wishes had been granted. I needed a companion and life had sent back my best friend. Also, contrary to what I had believed, Sakshi had not changed at all.

After gorging on the scrumptious dinner prepared by mom, Sakshi and I moved to my room. I noticed that I had really enjoyed my meal after a long time. Undoubtedly, it was

Sakshi's effect. Good friends don't let the miseries fog around you for long. They always manage to make you smile. That's what Sakshi's mere presence was doing to me. I requested her to stay for the night and she agreed right away.

'So, what is up with you? How is Bengaluru? Do you like that place? And tell me, why have you changed your look?' I began, throwing a series of questions at her.

'Bengaluru is an awesome place. My life has become all the more exciting there. My college is great and this look is my attempt to appear a bit more professional. However, there is another thing that is far more important than my look. I have found someone there,' she said, winking at me.

'What?' I asked, smiling in wonderment.

'Yes, ours is a very different story. His name is Raghav. I will tell you everything in detail but first, I need to know what's happening in your life. Did anything different happen in all these months?' she asked, very keenly, totally unaware of the fact that my life had turned upside down.

'Yeah, but not in a positive light,' I replied vaguely.

'What do you mean? What happened? And by the way, I did notice stress and anxiety on your face when you walked in. Was it due to work pressure?' she began, sounding concerned as she touched my hand lightly.

I looked at her but didn't say anything. She prodded and I realized that her unexpected return had a purpose. She was the only friend who could listen to me and help me get answers to the all questions that were haunting me since the day I last spoke to Maira.

"So basically, it started when I joined Biztech..."

❖

'And, since then I have been feeling so weird. I cannot focus on anything, neither at work nor at home. My mind has stopped functioning. It is very frustrating and it irritates me more because I can't figure out why I am feeling this way,' I said, explaining everything that had happened. By the time I was done speaking, I had tears in my eyes.

She listened to me closely. I pleaded her to help me figure out my complex feelings. She was quiet initially. And then, suddenly, she hit me with a pillow in my face.

'Idiot! Why didn't you tell me all this before? So much was happening in your life and you didn't even call me once? Why?' she asked angrily. I realized that being my friend, she had got a little offended that I kept all this from her.

'I thought you were already busy dealing with a new city, new college and new people. I didn't want to add to your problems,' I said, trying to explain my situation to her.

'What? Are you insane! Friends don't bother each other, ever. Tell me, had you been in my place, wouldn't you have listened to me? How could you think like this? Did we stop being friends? Ashna, distances don't separate friends, people do,' she replied softly, patting and rubbing my arm where she had pinched a moment ago.

'I am sorry. I know I made a big mistake not telling you all this before and as you can see, I am already paying for it. But, I need you now Sakshi. No one knows me enough to help me out of this situation, please,' I said, feeling utterly apologetic.

'By the way, that girl Maira, she was a conniving bitch. Why did she ruin your friendship with Samar?' she asked in an acerbic tone.

'She is not a bitch, Sakshi. I guess whatever she did was for Aman, her best friend and I can understand,' I replied, smiling back sadly. I didn't understand why I defended her. Maybe, because I could relate to her on some level.

'Okay, but what was the need? If it wasn't Aman who asked her to do all that, then why did she do everything on her own? Also, if her purpose was to make you fall for Aman, then why did she ask Samar out? Anyway, just chuck her out and let's talk about you,' she said, hugging me with her warm embrace.

'What? What about me?' I replied.

'I mean, where you are on your feelings about Samar?' she spoke very earnestly.

'I guess at the same place as I was before. He is my best friend. That's it,' I replied vaguely.

'Ashna, are you serious? After all that has happened? Especially after everything that you've been feeling since Maira proposed Samar, are you telling me that he is still just a friend?' she replied, in a severe tone.

I just shrugged my shoulders at her. I didn't really have an answer to her question. Or perhaps, I was too afraid to admit what my heart was forcing me to admit. I needed someone's validation and Sakshi could help me with that.

'Ashna what are you looking for in a man you'd love?' she asked.

'I want a romantic love story with someone who knows me like no one does. Who can love me like no one else! And, who can do anything for bringing to life our fairy tale romance,' I replied.

'And is Samar any different from all those things you mentioned?' she asked in a matter-of-fact tone.

There it is. Exactly what I've been looking for. I want to believe in what you're saying Sakshi, but I'm too afraid. I can't lose him.

'No, Samar is everything that anyone can ever want, but we don't share any romantic spark. And if it does exist between us, then how come we have never found it?' I argued.

'He did, but you didn't. You have always denied it and you are still doing that,' she replied. I could sense that she was frustrated but I needed her to be patient. I was almost there.

'No, I am not in denial. Maybe, I'm just being practical. I mean, we have never even had a story, let alone a romantic one,' I replied, faking a laugh.

'Wow, do you know that you are running after a very unrealistic idea of love? You need to live in reality, Ashna. If you don't love him, then why did you sacrifice yourself and get into a false relationship with Aman? Why are you so afraid of losing him to Maira? What is this feeling that you have ever since you got to know about their relationship? Don't tell me you don't know, because you do. You are just fooling yourself because you're afraid. You just don't want to accept the fact that you are ardently in love with Samar,' she said straightforwardly.

She had hit the bull's eye. 'Yes, I love him,' I murmured with tear-filled eyes. It felt so peaceful to say that aloud. All the knots of my mind and body were being loosened and I could feel a sense of calmness entering my system. I knew nothing was more important to me than Samar. I had always loved him. The jealousy, insecurity, possessiveness, loneliness and a sense of loss without him, was all for love.

'What did you say?' she said, looking at me shocked.

'I love him. It has always been about love and not about just friendship. I realized it long ago, perhaps, when he visited me after my accident. In fact, that's why I broke up with Aman as I felt that I was being unfair to him. A few minutes ago, you had asked me what I longed for. I long for him. He is everything I want, but I took him for granted, and now he is happy with Maira. I don't want to break his heart once again. I want him to be happy with Maira,' I said, sobbing between my words.

I was breaking out of all my restrictions. 'Ashna, I'm so glad to hear that. You know we realize the value of someone only when that person goes away from us. I'm so happy for you,' she cried, hugging me tightly.

'I love him and I want to tell this to him. However, I restrain myself each time because of Maira. I know they must be very happy together. He has finally moved on, and I don't want to disturb him,' I said, pining away in my lover's sighs.

This was karma coming to me full circle.

'You drove him away from yourself. Now, all you can do is believe in the power of love. If it made you realize your feelings, then maybe, it will figure out a way to bring Samar back to you,' she said, trying to calm me.

I couldn't get better. Everything felt bleak.

Was this how our story was going to end?

I couldn't sleep. I kept staring at the ceiling, just like I had on the night of the graduation dinner when Samar had proposed me.

22

The Climax

Ashna

Two days later, my condition had worsened. Although Sakshi had helped me express my feelings, but I had become depressed and gloomy. I had to deal with the guilt of not realizing my love for him at the right time and for driving him away from me. It had disrupted my mental peace so much that I had to take a four-day leave from office. I hoped to be away from all the chaos.

However, I wasn't doing anything constructive sitting at home, except to sulk around all day. I was filled with regret, especially for turning down Samar's proposal on the night of the graduation dinner. I missed Samar more than ever. I couldn't understand how Samar had patiently waited for four years to tell me that he loved me because I was getting so impatient and apprehensive. I was dying to tell him, but I couldn't. After all, he was not entitled to my whims and fancies anymore.

I tried to combat my dismay as I sat down to watch a movie. I don't know why I chose *Made of Honor,* a movie that involved two best friends where the girl loved the guy, but the guy thought that they were friends until she asked him to be her maid of honour for her wedding.

Just like me, the guy realized that he loved the girl only when she was about to go away from him. He then, tried to win her back because he realized that they were soul mates who had met as best friends. Maybe that's why I watched this movie, because it was basically my life in a nutshell. The only difference was that I didn't even get a chance to stop my best friend from going away.

The climax had come and the guy was rushing to get to the girl.

Go, get her.

I prayed for the two characters, wishing them to get together. Of course, they had to because it was a movie. Simultaneously, I was also thinking about Samar and what he might have been doing with Maira.

Perhaps he's having a brunch with Maira and planning on what romantic thing they should do next.

It felt sick even thinking about it. Now I knew how Samar must have felt when I told him about my relationship with Aman. How stupid I was to do that!

I was immersed in these thoughts when someone rang the doorbell. As I opened the door, Sakshi stood in front of me, gaping at me with a wide smile on her face.

'What are you doing here?' I asked her, trying to sound excited.

'I have to give you a good news,' she replied, her eyes gleaming with happiness and enthusiasm.

'Tell me what is it?' I said, unaffected because no news was good enough for me. I settled back on my couch and resumed the movie. I didn't like the fact that she had disrupted the climax of my movie. At least somebody should have a happy ending.

'Samar is in Delhi,' she said, capturing all my attention.

I immediately hit the pause button and sat up straight, looking at her with wide eyes. 'What? Are you serious? How do you know?' I asked.

Suddenly, I felt rejuvenated and hopeful.

'I texted him on WhatsApp to congratulate him on his new relationship and that's when he told me that he was in Delhi,' she said, smiling at me.

That was my reality check. 'So what? Even if he is in Delhi, what can I do? He must have come here with Maira,' I replied, trying to sound indifferent.

'No, that's what I have come here to tell you. He is not in a relationship,' she said as I involuntarily jumped up with surprise and sat upright on the couch.

Did I hear that correctly? Samar is still single? How?

'What? Maira had asked him out? Did he turn her down? What happened?' I asked keenly.

'She asked him out and he agreed, but he didn't want to. Interestingly, she dumped him in the morning and left a letter for him in which she told him that she couldn't be in a relationship with him because he loved someone else,' she completed.

'What?' I was perplexed, 'How could she do this to him? I will call her and question her. She can't get away doing this to Samar,' I was enraged. After all that she had done, this was the final blow.

After a pause, I continued, 'But, who is Samar in love with?' I asked. My heart was throbbing as I waited for her to answer.

She smiled at me, 'Don't you already know the answer?' she winked.

I stared at her in disbelief. I couldn't believe that Samar still loved me, even after all that I had done to him. Sakshi's words felt like soothing raindrops on my face under scorching heat. Maybe, we were really soul mates because we were best friends.

'What shall I do, tell me Sakshi?' I asked nervously.

'You need to tell him that you love him or you can wait for him to confess his feelings.' She shrugged.

'No! I can't wait for him anymore. He has already done it enough times. Now it's my turn. It is time that I go to him to express my undying love for him,' I almost shouted.

I noticed that I was humming some romantic tunes in my mind. Suddenly, everything around me turned very filmi. I could feel violins and pianos playing in the background. With the excitement, all my sorrows and desperation withered away. Maybe that is why love is regarded as the most magical sentiment. It makes us do things that we have never done before.

'Ashna, if you want to tell him, I think you need to run. He came to Delhi for an interview which didn't go well, so he is returning to Mumbai. In fact,' she said and looked at her watch, 'He leaves in around an hour so you better hurry up!' she completed, encouraging me to seize the opportunity.

This pep talk was good good enough to give me jitters. 'I need to talk to him. I have to tell him everything before he leaves,' I said.

'When is he going? I mean, when is his flight leaving? Did he tell you anything?' I continued, thinking whether I would be able to pull off one of those classic airport endings.

'Flight? He is taking a train to Mumbai and that will leave soon from Nizamuddin station. Anyway, don't worry, I'll drive you there if you want,' she said.

I could feel adrenaline rushing in my veins. 'Okay, we can go to the railway station. Let's go Sakshi. I won't let him leave before he knows how much I love him.' I was starting to go towards my room to change so that I could get ready for the adventure. But, Sakshi stopped me right away.

'No! We don't have time for you to change. Let's leave right away,' she said as she held my hand and dragged me out of the house.

'Okay, but I need to take something,' I said, and rushed back into the house. I ran into my room and grabbed the precious thing that I was looking for. Then, we rushed to her car and hit the road.

I will write the perfect ending of my love story. I'll do what Simran did for Raj!

❖

As we were on the road, tackling the horrible Delhi traffic, various scenes of "chase-your-love-before-he-leaves" started to play in my head. I was nervous and thrilled at the same time. This was our romantic story that I had been waiting for!

We reached Nizamuddin station in an hour as Sakshi had contemplated. I had tried calling Samar from Sakshi's phone, but his number was switched off. We were starting to get worried as we had no clue about his train or platform.

Sakshi asked me to get out of the car and start looking for Samar while she parked the car. I agreed because I didn't want Samar to leave before I could meet him.

I took the precious thing that I had procured from my cupboard and started running in the direction of the main entrance of the railway station. All the people including the coolies, fellow passengers, taxi drivers, auto drivers and other people looked at me as if I was some crazy girl. However, I didn't care. Who could blame them? A confused looking girl running on the train station in her night pyjamas wasn't a regular sight for them.

I ran through the station and various platforms, jumping over suitcases and running past people, trying my best to find Samar in that crowd. Then, I decided to get to the main station, but for that I needed a platform ticket which could have delayed me. So, I decided to gate crash, hoping that my risk would finally pay off.

However, before I could continue with my adventure, I received a call from Sakshi. Thinking that she might have found Samar, I hurriedly answered her call.

'Where are you? Did you find Samar?' she asked.

'No, I thought that you had found him,' I replied, sounding disappointed.

'No, I haven't, but I think he prefers to wait at Comesum restaurant for his train, instead of standing at the platform. I guess you should take a look there,' she said.

Without thinking twice, I rushed towards Comesum. I ran inside it and trying to catch my breath, looked around. Everyone was staring at me, and amongst those strange stares, I found that familiar one that I had longed for. There he was, my Samar! He sat there with Kartik. Our eyes finally met.

❖

Samar

A week had gone by since that strange incident with Maira.

I was back in Delhi, and had almost forgotten about it. It was surprising that I did not miss Maira even though we had met multiple times. In fact, I wouldn't even remember about her except for the times when those questions arose in my head. However, once I was in Delhi, it was easy to brush them aside, because I was back home to my family and friends.

My new job at Little Spot Publications had also begun. I had resigned from Med-a-Door right after speaking to Jyotsana. I absolutely loved working at Little Spot Publications. I loved my office, its creative interiors and the wonderful people who were always eager to help me out. The beautiful illustrations around me sparked off my creativity and enhanced my craft. It was probably my passion for cartooning that made me enjoy my workplace. Life was going smoothly until that adventurous day.

❖

I was at home, working on an assignment for my first project when I received a call from Kartik. He was waiting outside my house to meet me. Without giving me a reason, he instructed me to come out. I tried to tell him that I was working on my first project and was busy, but he wouldn't budge.

When I went outside, he opened the door and gestured me to sit in his car. I sat and without saying anything, he started to drive. It was hard to decipher his behaviour.

'Could you at least tell me where we're going?' I asked, in a huff.

'Nizamuddin railway station'

'What? Why? Are we going to pick up someone?' I asked totally confused.

'No, I just want to go to Comesum. I have to tell you something important,' he said plainly.

'Are you crazy? I had some urgent work to finish and you called me out. Now you're telling me that you want to go to Comesum?' I shouted.

'Samar, please relax! I really need to tell you something important, but I can't talk until we reach Comesum,' he replied, shrugging his shoulders.

'What is the matter with you? Why Comesum when we could have gone to some nearby cafe? What is so happening about that place?' I said, clearly irritated by his juvenile behaviour. I guess I was more annoyed because Kartik wasn't reacting at all.

'It has good food,' he replied vaguely.

'Bro, give me a break! We are going all the way to Nizamuddin's Comesum for good food. Why? Are you out of your mind?' I said enraged. I didn't understand why he was being so weird and unreasonable.

'Samar, relax yaar! Once we will be there, you too will love its food,' he said

To curb my anger, I took out my phone and started to surf Facebook. Suddenly, Kartik snatched my phone away and switched it off.

'Why did you take my phone?' I yelled.

Why is he irritating me so much?

'You have come with me, not with your phone,' he replied, sounding like a possessive girlfriend.

What has happened to this guy?

'By the way, you know two or three weeks ago, Ashna broke up with Aman?' he said, out of the blue.

'What? She broke up with him? Why? Did he do something?' I launched a series of questions at him.

'No, she just broke up. I don't know, but I just know they are not together anymore,' he said, rekindling a flame of hope that was once extinguished inside me. I was reminded of Maira who said that Ashna loved me. But I returned to reality as I realized that she hadn't contacted me even after her break-up, which meant that there was nothing left between us.

'Why are you telling me this? It's their personal matter,' I said, trying to sound as if I was unaffected by it.

'I thought you might be interested in knowing what Ashna was up to,' he retorted.

'No, I am not,' I said bluntly.

Throughout the drive, I thought only about Ashna. I had not contacted her after coming to Delhi because I thought she was steady in her relationship, and now I got to know that she wasn't even in that relationship. Why?

I decided that I would ask her, but then I immediately dropped that idea because I didn't want her to feel that I was just lurking around for her to get out of that relationship.

As soon as we reached Comesum, I looked around to see if I could find anything special about that place, but I found nothing. Everything looked normal, except that most of its customers were railway passengers.

I gestured Kartik to order whatever delicious dish he wanted us to have, but to my dismay, he wasn't hungry anymore. I decided to be patient and wait with him.

'Okay, I get it. You are not hungry right now and that's fine, but at least tell me what did you want to share?' I asked him, very calmly.

'Yeah... that thing... I am sorry but you will have to wait for some time to know that,' he completed his statement quickly and started looking around as if he was searching for someone.

I couldn't help getting annoyed with him. It seemed as if he just wanted to waste my time, but why?

Has this guy totally lost it? First, he told me he was not hungry and now he is telling me that I will have to wait to know that important thing as well. Then what exactly are we doing here?

We remained seated for another fifteen minutes. We didn't even talk much, except when I requested him to give back my phone. But he didn't.

'That's it, I can't take it anymore. Tell me what are we doing here or I am leaving right now,' I said, getting up to leave.

'Fine! If you don't have any patience, then listen, actually...,' he had just begun stuttering when suddenly, a girl in pyjamas barged into the restaurant. Our attention turned towards her like everyone else's. It seemed funny until I looked at her closely and our eyes locked.

Ashna? What was she doing here? Did she come to receive someone? Why is she in her pyjamas?

I couldn't take my eyes off her. She started walking towards us, gasping for breath, but also managing to smile. Her eyes were sparkling and her face looked peaceful.

My heart was overjoyed to see her. I wanted to believe that she was mine. On the contrary, my mind intervened and I realized that it was wrong to jump to conclusions.

As she came to our table, Kartik and I stood up curiously. I was about to ask her what the matter was, but before I could have said anything, she came to me and hugged me tightly. It was the kind of hug that I had always craved for.

She didn't let go of me for a few seconds. I lost track of time myself, as if it was a dream.

'Thank god I found you. Thank god you haven't left for Mumbai yet. I want to tell you something,' she murmured in a heavy voice.

I am going to Mumbai? When? Why? And how come I don't know about it and she does?

'Listen,' I began to clarify, but Kartik gestured me to keep quiet. She let go of me and I noticed that Sakshi stood behind Ashna.

'Samar,' said Ashna kneeling down on one knee.

I just stared at her. I was frozen.

What is she about to do?

All the people in the restaurant, including the waiters, stopped whatever they were doing and turned to look at us, looking as baffled as I felt.

'I know I have always been mean to you. I did things that I shouldn't have, but you have always loved me. What can I say, I was so foolish. I am sorry Samar. I didn't realize what love was. I knew what friendship was and I tried to protect that, but I lost you in the process. Everything went haywire and you were gone. It was then that I realized that I could not live without you. I might meet new people, but no one can replace you Samar. I want you to be my eternal truth because Ashna is incomplete without Samar.

'I was afraid that our friendship would mess up if we fell in love, but now I realize that it's our friendship that made us fall in love,' she said, pausing to change from one knee to another.

'Being friends, we have always cared for each other more than lovers. We have tried to put each other before ourselves. Sometimes, I feel that maybe we exist only for each other. That's why I want us to be together because now, I understand that you were not just my best friend, but my soul mate. You are free to reject my proposal and I will understand, but—' she paused to take out something from her pocket and she held it up like a ring.

'You are the most precious thing to me and I want to keep you forever. I have always loved you and will always love you. Please be mine,' she completed.

I was shocked. Ashna was holding up the peepal leaf that I had given to her while proposing on the night of our graduation party. I was speechless. It was a lot to process. For a second, I thought that everything was an illusion. However, I couldn't deny the tears in her eyes which reflected the sincerity of her confession. I just kept staring at her in disbelief.

The most awaited moment of my life had finally come true. My best friend, whom I had eternally loved, had just proposed to me. Overwhelmed by all those emotions, I managed to smile.

I was lost in her eyes. I think I was right to believe in destiny. Whatever belonged me was destined to come at the right moment. If Ashna had said yes to my proposal on the night of graduation dinner, she wouldn't have realized how much she loved me. Or perhaps, I would still be squandering away my time, not realizing that I wanted to be a cartoonist. However, my destiny was at work all this time and everything fell into place.

'Samar, you can take as much time as you want, but it's hurting my knee a little,' Ashna spoke in a squeaky little voice.

'I can't believe it!' I exclaimed as I held her hand to help her stand up. Then I looked into her innocent eyes and entwined my fingers in hers, as I said, 'Ashna, I love you too. I have loved you ever since we met. I will always be yours. I promise, my love won't ever change. I promise that from now on, we will be better friends than before. We will always be there for each other,' I said, choking on my words.

We shared an emotional moment soaked in romance. She jumped and hugged me intensely. It was so intense that I almost lost my balance for a second. I even lifted her up a little. I looked around and saw Kartik and Sakshi with broad smiles on their faces. As I put her down, I kissed on her forehead.

'By the way, I was never going back to Mumbai because I have a job in Delhi as a cartoonist. Why did you feel that I was going to Mumbai?' I asked Ashna, when we had somewhat controlled our excitement.

'What? Sakshi said that she spoke to you. You were leaving for Mumbai today. That's why I came running to meet you,' she replied in haste, catching up on her breath after a lot of excitement.

'No! I didn't have any such plans. In fact, Kartik brought me here because... Oh, you brought me here for this?' I spoke, soon making sense of everything. All the pieces of the puzzles fell into place, giving rise to the most beautiful reality of my life.

Kartik and Sakshi looked at each other.

'This was our little contribution to your love story,' said Sakshi, grinning and winking at us.

Epilogue

One Year Later

Ashna

We were sitting at our favourite café, Cheeros. Kartik had asked us to meet there. He wanted to tell us something, but he hadn't come yet.

We wished that Sakshi could also join us, but she was back in Bengaluru and busy with her office work.

I was busy laughing, looking at the funny face that Samar had made because I had ordered quesadilla, his least favourite dish. I knew he didn't like it and that's why I had ordered it, as a revenge for making me eat pesto sauce pasta last week.

Yes, we irritate each other sometimes because along with being two people who are madly in love with each other, we are also best friends.

We have a perfect relationship together. It's not as if we don't fight, but our mutual understanding and comfort with each other ensures that we overcome all the obstacles. Being with Samar feels right in every way because he was always an integral part of my life. He taught me a lot about unconditional love.

If you refrain yourself from falling in love with your best friend, then you are missing out on a chance to be in the best relationship of your life.

Initially, I was afraid that I may lose Samar, but our relationship has made me realize that friendship solidifies a bond as both these connections are incomplete without each other. His unfaltering belief in fate has encouraged me to embrace my own destiny.

Destiny will bring what belongs to us eventually, at the right time. We were destined to be together and that worked the best for us, not just personally but also professionally.

Samar had finally become a successful cartoonist. He got five permanent columns in four different magazines of Little Spot Publications, apart from other freelancing projects from other publications and newspapers. People loved his cartoons and the biggest fans of his work, of course apart from me, were his parents. Although they were once worried about his career but now, they boast about him in front of their relatives. It was such a proud achievement for him.

Samar could have made more money had he chosen architecture, but that wouldn't have given him contentment, peace and appreciation that he received from cartooning. Architecture was never his calling. Rather, it was my calling.

My Kausani hotel project was nearly complete and the owners were more than happy. However, I am not the only one to take credit. The entire team at Biztech, especially Aman and Rajat, had worked day and night to make it a success story. Rajat was still the same, nothing had changed about him. After Maira left, we hardly interacted. Aman and I just shared a professional relationship now. Perhaps, he understood that we were never made for each other.

Samar told me everything that had happened between him and Maira in Mumbai. He even showed me that letter which Maira had left for him. When I read that, I was sure that Maira loved Aman. Whatever it may have been, I don't know if she ever told him about it. However, we don't hold any grudges against Maira. In fact, we are thankful to her because she made us realize how much we loved each other.

I noticed that Samar's gaze was fixated on me, 'What? Is there something on my face?' I asked.

'Yes, your beautiful eyes. Did I ever tell you that admiring them is my favourite activity. I love you, I mean… your eyes. I mean you entirely,' he replied.

'I already know that. Do you think I haven't noticed it for an entire year?' I said, and gave him a naughty smile. 'By the way, where is Kartik, and why did he call us here?'

'Wherever he is, let him be. At least he is giving us ample quality time in our favourite café,' he said, as he lovingly held my hand.

'I can come back later if I am interrupting,' Kartik's voice cut through my happy thoughts.

'No! Hi Kartik,' I replied, embarrassed as I retracted my hand from Samar's. He and Samar passed each other a smile while Kartik sat next to me. We kept staring at him, waiting for him to spill the important news.

'I wanted to talk to you guys because I think something has happened to me. Although, I am not sure, but I think I am in love,' he said, as we looked at him and then at each other excitedly.

'What? When did this happen?' said Samar.

And thus began another tale of love.

A Note from the Author

Dear reader,

Thank you for choosing this book and embarking on the journey of friendship and love with Ashna and Samar. This story is very close to my heart and is inspired by a real life friendship that went through a journey of emotional confusion, heartbreaks and love over the years. That's why, it was an endearing and emotional experience for me to write down every single scene.

I hope this story touched your heart too, and reminded you of the sweet memories with your best friend or the deep love you have had for someone.

Tell me honestly, in this beginning to Samar and Ashna's 'happily ever after', were you left with some questions?

Why did Maira never share anything about herself with Ashna or Samar?
Why did she deceive them with her shenanigans?

Did she do it for her best friend Aman?
Did Aman ask her to do all that? Was he a part of her plan too?
And when Maira was about to kiss success, why did she give up and leave that letter with Samar? What changed her mind?

Ashna and Samar never got the answers to these questions because they could never find out more about Maira. She remained a mystery.

But, everyone is living a different story. Maira also, has a story of her own. She is going to answer all these questions for sure. Let's explore it together someday.